Praise for *The Perturbation of O*

"Joseph Peterson's whirling, twirling prose winds us deeper into the comical and often dark nature of fame, obsession, art; what it means to be truthful to yourself, and if that's even something worthy of pursuing anymore. This intoxicating two-way conversation hits upon themes familiar to Gen-Xers who came of age carrying the weight of slacker culture. But rather than writing another generational celebration of familiar tropes, Peterson peels them back to reveal their absurdist underbelly. This is gripping psychological stuff for readers interested in the dark corners of how art gets made and remade and remade again."

—**Mark Guarino,** author, *Country and Midwestern:*
Chicago in the History of Country Music and the Folk Revival

"With his signature wit and wisdom, Joseph Peterson's latest offering is a bittersweet exploration of the highs and lows encountered along the border of art and commerce. *The Perturbation of O* deftly lays bare the heavy toll that fame exacts from the creative soul."

—**Giano Cromley,** author, *American Mythology*

"*The Perturbation of O* paints a profoundly real picture of the way artists and writers live inside their heads. Much like antiheroes Gideon and Regina, we creative types are a tribe unto ourselves: outsiders, outlanders, misunderstood misfits. Products of American romanticism, we imagine someday somewhere someone will swoop down and lift us up to art heaven, saving our souls and sanctifying our tortured artwork. Then, along comes Joseph Peterson with his latest twisted parable."

—**Ed Rath,** artist

"Joseph Peterson, like his character Regina, is also a 'painter of light' . . . with his mastery of language and dialogue, he is constantly bringing the reader back to the subtle, spiritual underpinnings that are the fabric of story and life."

—**Robert Silverman,** jazz pianist and composer

"Peterson draws these characters with intensity, compassion, and humor. He has an orbital camera, taking snapshots of every aspect of their stories as they obsess over the past and over their fate, each time finding some new detail that pokes and twinges their memories with regret in the case of Gideon and wonder in the case of Regina."
—**Mike Brehm,** artist

"Whether channeling Blake or dancing with Oprah, this hypnotic torrent of words slips under the hood of the creative combustion engine to reveal all the leaking oil and rusted pistons."
—**Jon Langford,** musician, The Mekons

"I read Joseph Peterson's book in one sitting when it came in the post. I found it extremely engaging and tangent to many of my own personal aesthetic interests. The writing seemed woven together like a long prose poem. The story had a feeling like waves coming onto a shoreline, the high-low feeling of deep concerns and shallow cultural touchstones were fascinating, as if the author wrestled with his own past confessions as a terrible mistakenness. Yes, it's an unusual journey, but it made me wonder about why it's so difficult to tell the truth even in fictional literature. Confessions are always enticing, and this is a juicy tale.

Put more concisely, the story held my attention and hit many points of reference that kept me engaged. The flavor was very contemporary but set in a very specific place and moment that oscillates with ebb and flow of the remembrances. It's sexy without being explicit, a bit fantastic but grounded in the author's self-doubt. Slack is just so then and there."
—**Frank Gaard,** editor, *Artpolicecomics*

THE PERTURBATION OF O

The
Perturbation
of O

Joseph G. Peterson

UNIVERSITY OF IOWA PRESS | IOWA CITY

University of Iowa Press, Iowa City 52242
Copyright © 2025 by Joseph G. Peterson
uipress.uiowa.edu
Printed in the United States of America

Cover design by Kathleen Lynch
Text design and typesetting by April Leidig

This is a work of fiction. Unless otherwise indicated, all the names,
characters, businesses, places, events, and incidents in this book
are either the product of the author's imagination or used in a
fictitious manner. Any resemblance to actual persons, living
or dead, or actual events is purely coincidental.

Printed on acid-free paper

Library of Congress Cataloging-in-Publication Data
Names: Peterson, Joseph G., author.
Title: The Perturbation of O / Joseph G. Peterson.
Identifiers: LCCN 2024018811 (print) | LCCN 2024018812 (ebook) |
ISBN 9781685970024 (paperback; acid-free paper) |
ISBN 9781685970031 (ebook)
Subjects: LCGFT: Novels.
Classification: LCC PS3616.E84288 P47 2025 (print) |
LCC PS3616.E84288 (ebook) | DDC 813/.6—dc23/eng/20240812
LC record available at https://lccn.loc.gov/2024018811
LC ebook record available at https://lccn.loc.gov/2024018812

For Linda and Mark Amdur,
with love and gratitude.
L'Chaim

Ecce deus fortior me, qui veniens dominabitur mihi.
Here is a deity stronger than I; who, coming, shall rule over me.

—Dante

La Vita Nuova by Dante Alighieri. Translated by Dante Gabriel Rosetti.

She noticed me before I noticed her and when I first set eyes on her I still didn't notice her because she was still to me, at that point, just a random person standing in line behind me at the coffee shop while I reached in my pocket for my wallet, but by the time I had set eyes on her nodding my head to her, briefly, that I had seen and therefore acknowledged her existence, she not only noticed me, taking me all in with those large dark eyes of hers but she had sized me up and made some assessment of what had become of me in the seventeen years since we had last seen each other; she had noticed me, sized me up, and as I later came to understand, she had seen straight through me while I, innocently enough, was still ordering my coffee at the counter of the coffee shop. And yes, I'll have cream with that coffee, I said to the woman who was taking my order. And yes, please, an extra sugar. And also, I'll take a banana and a blueberry scone.

After I had ordered my breakfast at the coffee shop—Your name sir, the cashier asked, Gideon, I told her; We will call you, Gideon, when your order is ready—I took a seat near a window and I opened a book written by the grandson of an old Kentucky gentleman I knew, a book that told the story of his, the grandson's, tormenting years-long illness, his critically necessary relationship with his dog, and his subsequent, almost miraculous recovery, brought on by that pet relationship. It was memoir, which he promised told a happy story, man/dog/cure, because he was in a good place now and that was part of the story his book told, a book that was still with the publisher and that he had asked me to blurb, and I had wanted to spend the morning perusing his man/dog/cure book so that I might offer him a favorable blurb and thereby return a favor to an old friend, the Kentucky gentleman, and that's when I looked out the window of the coffee shop at the morning light that filled the space beyond the window where there was a pretty garden, and which that spring morning moved me in a way that left me speechless because the trees were just budding, and the cherry blossoms were in full bloom, and the magnolias were just opening, and improbably large bumblebees were buzzing and bumbling in the wet and preternaturally cool spring air, and it had been my habit back then, whenever I encountered the natural beauty of a morning light that filled my heart with joy, to close my eyes and try to meditate. No, "meditate" isn't exactly the right word. What I had attempted to do whenever I closed my eyes back then was to hold back the emotion of joy that was filling my heart because of the beauty of the morning light and threatening to cause me to openly weep, which is something I often did in public during those days, but with eyes closed, I also tried to hold inside myself the moment of beauty that the morning light had induced, to hold it close to my heart or on the inside of my eyelids before the moment and the light with it vanished forever, and while I sat in my chair that morning in the coffee shop with my eyes closed trying to stem and hold the emotion of beauty I heard my name, Gideon, called out and I opened my eyes and there she was in front of me holding my cup of coffee and my banana and my blueberry scone, and she said, I grabbed these for you, Gideon, because when the woman at the counter called your name, you were sitting here with your eyes closed and when I told the cashier that I knew you, and that I would bring them to you, she said okay.

You know me, I asked, surprised, still unable to process what was happening because I was still in a sort of trance-like state and I had been jolted out of my trance-like state by her voice that I recognized but which I could not place, and whenever I was jolted in such a way, I could feel my heart rhythm quite strong in my chest, and still waiting for my heart to still, she told me that her name was Regina and that we had known each other seventeen years ago, and how time flies, and can you remember, Gideon, and I know that's your name because that's what you told the woman at the counter, but can you remember, Gideon, the last time we met? Do you even know who I am? And before I let you answer any of these questions, let me tell you how surprised I am to see you after all these years. I never thought I would see you again, and though I'm certain you've forgotten me, I certainly haven't forgotten you. And when she said this to me, she put so much pressure on me to remember who it was, who was this woman who was now suddenly standing in front of me, that out of the blue I had said, Is it Regina? The painter?

Bravo, she said, clapping her hands. It is Regina the painter.

Regina the painter, I said, surprised. Not only had seventeen years elapsed since the last time we had seen each other, but it had been nearly seventeen years since I had even thought about her. And while she stood in front of me, I smiled at her because she looked virtually unchanged since the last time I had seen her, she still wore her close-cropped hair and looking upon her as she looked frankly upon me, I felt it again like I had felt it the first time I had ever seen her, I felt her brutal honesty, and it shocked me a bit to feel the brutal honesty of her gaze upon me but it also comforted me, because I realized when I looked upon her that in my life I had never encountered someone as openly willing to be brutally honest, but I had also realized that in my life that was the one thing in my life that had been missing: an encounter with someone who was willing to be brutally honest with the likes of me. I realized while looking at her that her seeming willingness to be brutally honest and, more to the point, brutally honest with me was something that I had been looking for my whole life, and facing or rather confronting her brutal honesty head-on felt unbelievably like I had suddenly arrived in my own promised land.

To say that she was virtually unchanged is preposterous, really, because everyone, and I don't care who you are, changes over time, and over seventeen years though it can seem like it passes in the blink of an eye, yet no one remains unchanged over such a period of time, and so it was preposterous when I said to her, It's just like old times, Regina, you haven't changed a bit, which caused her to laugh, preposterously, and she said,

And you haven't changed either, Gideon. You look exactly the same.

No, I confessed to her. I've gotten fat and dissolute. I would tell you that I've lost my way, but that would suggest that I was on some sort of path in the so-called sun-dappled wood, and that I had veered off the path at some point and had gotten lost, but the fact is, I wandered directly into the woods sun-dappled or dark though they might be, and I made my way into the woods without knowing where I was headed, or what might become of me and it is in this long walkabout called my life, a walkabout, I should add, that was a walkabout to nowhere, where you have captured me unawares, and speechless.

You still talk a bunch of shit, Gideon, but it's still nice to see you again. And I seem to recall you were fat and dissolute and without direction even back in the day. Then she smiled at me rather slyly and said, The King of Slack!

Are you living in Chicago? I asked.

Did I ever leave? she said.

Last time I saw you, Regina, you had a studio on the South Side of Chicago, on Sixty-First Street and Dorchester, are you still at that studio? Are you still painting? I should know if you are still painting, but I admit, I've lost contact with you.

Or interest . . . Regina said.

I've lost interest in almost everybody from back then, I confessed. I always had a problem finding interest and holding it.

I'm still a painter, if that means anything to you but it probably doesn't, and I still have my own studio, though I relocated to my new studio not long after I left college. My new space—not so new actually, even though that's what I call it—but my new space is just north of Chinatown on the Chicago River. You should come by and visit some time. I read your book by the way, *Gideon's Confession*, Gideon, where you wrote about us such as we were back then, and though, overall, I wasn't pleased with what you wrote, I can say this to your credit: in all my years as a painter, these seventeen years, no one has written a more accurate portrait of my art than you have, Gideon, and I thank you for that.

I don't write books anymore, Regina, I told her. I also don't remember what I said of you in that book I had written.

The book I had written, *Gideon's Confession*, was, up until that point, the sole accomplishment of my life. It told the brief story of my final year at the University of Chicago where I had squandered my time not participating in classes, not planning for my future, but where I had gone about squandering funds that my uncle sent me on a monthly basis, it was a memoir I had initially titled *The Ark of Disquiet*, but my publisher had forced me to settle on a new title that suggested the confessional nature of the book, for in my book there was even talk of Catholic confession, and the publication of my book happened in the era before memoirs went mainstream and of course Augustine's *Confession* written at the end of the fourth century CE still hung heavy over books spoken with the formal "I," and so I was encouraged to change *The Ark of Disquiet* to *Gideon's Confession*, which, against my better judgment, I conceded, and after I had sent the book to the publisher under the new title, and after the publisher had agreed to publish the book, and after I had signed and put back in the mailbox the contract for book publication, I regretted immediately not only ever having written that book, but I also regretted sending it off to the publisher to get published, and I had regretted most of all having signed the contract, which put me in a legal relationship with my publisher that made the publishing of my so-called confession an almost forgone conclusion.

I've given more things up in my life, Regina, than I've taken up, I told her.

Are you still receiving checks from your uncle?

No. He's dead unfortunately.

And do you ever hear from Claire?

No, I told Regina. I lost track of Claire as well. The publication of my stupid book ended most of my relationships. The nightmare of my book, the whole Oprah Winfrey saga that ensued, the Broadway hit musical based on my book by the producer who had launched *Man of La Mancha* . . . "To dream the impossible dream". . . which was based less on my book and more on my antics on *The Oprah Winfrey Show* and then the cultish movie musical *The Slacker King*, which was based even less on my book and more on the Broadway hit musical, all of these things, the whole nightmare never seemed like it was going to end. I blush to recall it all before you now, Regina. And all the stupid fame that rained down on me like some sticky substance that I couldn't get off me and all of the problems that book and the ancillary spinoffs caused me. The headaches, the nightmares, the failed relationships. The recrimination. The social ostracization . . . So when you, Regina, call me the Slacker King it makes me want to puke. Also, that we were dubbed because of my book the

Slacker Generation but this was not good for me or for any of us. I shouldn't have named names. I shouldn't have written the book much less published it. I wish I could say it all never happened. At some point in my life, let's say some point in the middle when I was already lost, I got a brief note from Claire who had somehow figured out where I was living and she penned a note to me which I actually received and in that note she said, more or less, that she was a person without regrets, and that she never looked back but always looked ahead, but that, after the publication of my book, wherein I had detailed the particulars of our relationship, which was ultimately a failed relationship, and more, since I hadn't even disguised her identity or the identities of other persons in the book, and since our relationship had been acted in the oblivion of unrecorded time and vanishing memory, it had not only surprised her that I thought that our paltry relationship and she used that word, "paltry," but that our paltry relationship brief and forgettable as it so definitely was, nevertheless merited a booklike memoir in which none of the small petty details of that relationship were omitted, and she queried me in her letter, which I still have, saying, who was I of all people to think that I was justified in writing a book about a private relationship between two people that was carried on in good faith, to think that not only must a relationship like ours, paltry as it was, merit such treatment in print, and who was I, furthermore, to think that there was a market for such a memoir, and furthermore, was the whole point of the relationship merely to produce fodder for a memoir, and if so, then the relationship was necessarily a disingenuous affair, because while she came to me with the best of intentions, I came to her with a motive of subterfuge. And in that letter, which I still retain, I told Regina that morning in the coffee shop, Claire pointed out that not only was my motive with her, Claire, one of subterfuge based on the evidence of my book, but it had sunk and destroyed the better and more beautiful relationship that she had with her dear friend Regina, who, after the brief affair that I had had with Regina, and which Regina in her brutal honesty had disclosed to Claire, had thereby caused the end of the relationship between Claire and Regina. And as a postscript, of which there were several, which I will enumerate if you wish to hear more of this story, I told Regina, Claire had told me that Regina was the most searingly original artist she had ever had the good fortune to meet, and for a brief time, she and Regina had been best of friends, but my brief fling with Regina, which was (1) selfish, (2) hurtful, and (3) you are such an asshole/jackass for having perpetrated such a fling, but because of that fling, I now know of Regina only what I'm able to read of her in all the notices that I find relating to her art career; and postscript two: Did you know that Regina had artwork included in the Whitney Biennial? And postscript three: Did you know that Regina has won a Guggenheim? And postscript four: Did you know that Regina has also won a MacArthur Genius fellowship? And what has become of you, Gideon? All you did was write that stupid book called *Gideon's Confession* that no one really cared about except for me, and I only cared about it because I never wanted to be memorialized in some guy's book, especially some guy with whom I was having sex.

And then, of course, there was first the Broadway hit musical, *The Slacker King*, produced by the same guy who

9

produced "To Dream the Impossible Dream," *Man of La Mancha*, both of which, the treacly song and the sappy musical based on my book, were to my mind eminently forgettable but then there was the movie musical based on the Broadway musical of my book, *Gideon's Confession*, also called *The Slacker King*, which was a cult hit, unfortunately, and a permanent stain on American culture but its cultish permanence has permanently dubbed all of those I named in my book slackers and losers, when in point of fact I may have been the only one of the group who can be so characterized and of course, insofar as the Slacker King became famously lampooned so too were all of us lampooned and I suppose I am to blame for all of that. What else can I say? Sorry?

That's more or less what I told Regina that morning in the coffee shop when she brought me my banana and scone, and the thing is, Regina, who recognized me immediately, didn't have to bring me my banana and scone, instead she could have followed me in line at the cashier, ordered her mocha latte, and proceeded out the door and back into the world and thereby she could have left me alone to follow the quiddity of my own peculiar behavior, which was a behavior centered on processing the sensory data that was coming into my system all the time while dwelling also on my own internal emotional system. I was always searching for ways to process the beauty of the world, or rather the beauty of the light of the world which invariably, as it had just moments earlier staring out into that garden, nearly brought me to tears; she could have let me sit alone and cry over the beauty while going on her way, but that morning, she chose instead to order her mocha latte, and rather than proceeding out the door and back into the world, she chose to bring me my morning breakfast while I sat in the chair by the window enjoying the vision that I was able to hold somewhere between the backside of my eyelids and the backside of my brain where I'm able to both see and imagine things, the beauty and splendor of the morning light as it shone in the sublime and beauteous green quietude of the garden just outside the café window where an overlarge bumblebee in an almost comical manner flew about the different flower cups trying to find nectar and in the process had collected on its forearms and legs the dark yellow powdery pollen that it would unwittingly bring to some other flower cup in the garden and, Here, Gideon, I brought you these things from the counter. Do you remember me? And What of Claire? Have you heard from Claire?

I heard from Claire, I told Regina, not long after I published an utterly forgettable and stupid memoir called *Gideon's Confession* seventeen years ago. It was the first and last time I heard from her since we ended things.

Your book, Gideon, Regina said, was neither stupid nor forgettable. It was heartbreaking and beautiful and I've memorized whole tracts of it.

Oh really? So you read my book?

I did, Regina said. And though I said what I just said about it being beautiful, heartbreaking, and utterly unforgettable, I didn't particularly care for your characterization of anyone in the book who I happened to know and that includes primarily your representation of Claire, and even more your representation of me and of our fling, but regardless, in that book you did write of my artwork, and in my whole career these seventeen years and after all of these accolades I can honestly say that no one had written more incisively of my artwork than you did in your memoir, Gideon. In fact, I'll have you know, Regina said to me, that it wasn't an exaggeration to say that the publication of your book, *Gideon's Confession*, and the notoriety that your book, *Gideon's Confession*, has caused, and she paused a moment to look me in the eyes, and I looked back into those large dark eyes of hers, and I saw an almost mirthful expression on her face that was both full of warmth and completely honest in the way that Regina was capable of being completely honest, Did I say the "notoriety" that your book caused or should I rephrase that and say the small bit of notoriety or rather the small "sensation" that your book, *Gideon's Confession*, caused upon publication, but it was your book's splash in which you described better than anyone before or since has been able to describe my work, but it was your descriptions of my work in your work, *Gideon's Confession*, that was partly responsible for the rebirth of my career as an artist, a painter of brushstroke. Your book jumpstarted my painting career which had stalled not soon after you and I had had our tryst, and once jump-started which occurred in my new studio, I have been on an unbroken tear painting my own notorious canvases featuring the letter *O* these last seventeen years. I have committed myself wholeheartedly to my artwork, to the point where if you were to ask me what I am, I would tell you that I am an artist, and then if you were to ask me what I am not, I would tell you that I am not a person with a life outside my studio and my artwork. And I owe it all to you, Gideon, Regina said, even though, I must say, I'll never forgive you for portraying in graphic detail the night you and I had sex and which was graphically represented in the movie musical version of your book, *The Slacker King*.

What? How? I said, eating my banana while she rambled on. I pulled the scone from its wrapping paper and then I folded the banana peel into the wrapping paper and readied it for the trash. Then I bit into my scone, which was very tasty. Then I said to Regina, How did my book, which, by the way, I should tell you, I honestly regret not only publishing, but I also regret writing, but how did my book cause you to "jump-start," as you say, your career as an artist?

At this point I confessed to her that not only did I regret publishing my book, but that I also regretted writing it, and if it was any consolation to her, I actually don't even remember writing the book, and I only remotely remember publishing the book, and since the book was written and published I have done everything in my power to forget the whole crazy experience and pretend that it never happened, so that on crazy occasions, rare though they be, when someone approaches me to engage with me on my book, "Your book!" they'll say, transformed my life, but I will almost always inevitably say to them, the god's honest truth: What book are you talking about?

Your book, they'll say, *Gideon's Confession*!

How can my book have changed your life, when I myself don't even remember having written the book, much less can I even recall what the book was about, because as far as I can tell writing that book was the stupidest most worthless exercise I have ever brought myself to do, and having done it, now all I can hope to do is to forget it.

You underestimate yourself, Gideon, Regina said to me, as you always have. Your book changed my life as well.

How so?

It was your description of my artwork, which, as I said, no one has ever come close to matching. I remember you described me in your book as having "jackboots and butch hair," which is true, and I remember how you represented our sex that night, which, had someone asked me to represent it, I might have put it differently, but I saw, through your eyes, me, and seeing me through your eyes, I came to understand how other men, also having sex with me, might also see me. In fact, after your book was published, and after it had become a minor sensation, even I perhaps by the powers of your description had also become a bit of a minor sensation with a variety of sexual partners who wanted to try and duplicate the sex that you had written about in your book, *Gideon's Confession*, that we had had; but that was not the thing that changed my life so completely, what changed my life utterly was your description of my work, which you described as, and I can remember your exact words, because I have a good memory for such things, you wrote:

"She painted huge canvases of empty rooms filled with the most beautiful light imaginable. It was a 'light at the end of the tunnel' kind of light. A 'light that you see when you die and go to heaven' kind of light. Ask her what she painted, and she'd tell you, I paint light. But when you saw one of her pictures it was clear she was attempting nothing short of depicting some sort of celestial bliss. The beauty of the light in her pictures was so urgent and raw, it produced a lump in my throat."

Do you remember writing that, Gideon?

I don't remember writing it, I told Regina, because I believed if I was going to engage with Regina, then there was only one way to engage with her, I needed to be brutally honest, and so I told her, I don't remember writing those words, and as I said already, I very much regret writing that stupid memoir and I regret even more publishing that stupid memoir, because it didn't do anything for me other than to make me a hero to a bunch of anonymous fans who loved the book, and essentially a pariah to everyone in the book whom I had represented and also whom I had loved dearly, but that being said, if I did write that about your paintings then I meant it. I do recall quite vividly the beauty, the heart-sucking, breathtaking beauty of your artwork, Regina, and even now if I close my eyes I can see your paintings that hung in your studio some seventeen years ago, and I remember thinking that neither J.M.W. Turner in his late phase, those grand canvases collected at the Tate in London, nor the best work of Monet, the late water lilies, for instance, had anything on what you seemed capable of with a brush in hand, and sometimes even, when I do think back on those days, I told Regina, if I remember anything at all, and I confess that I remember very little from those days but the memory of your paintings is one of the few things that I retain of those times: the memory of those paintings in your studio on Sixty-First Street and Dorchester, and I am still grateful for those memories of your artwork and your former workspace.

Do you want me to put on some jackboots, Gideon? So we can give it another roll? I do say you talk a bunch of rot. Why do you loathe yourself so much, Gideon?

I don't loathe myself, I told Regina. I live in the moment, is all. I try to let go of the past, and I try to let go of those who were with me in the past, and I'm not particularly keen on thinking about the future, but sitting here, on this stool, looking through the window at the garden, and we both paused and looked out into the garden, and the green bursting vegetive and flowering state of the garden, the bursting magnolias, the roses, those bumblebees bumbling around, and here if you look closely, I told Regina, at this garden and I don't mean, just look closely, but if you look into that garden as if you too were alien to a human point of view, if you try to occupy it, blithely unaware of the human point of view, like those sparrows twittering in the bush, or the pollen-heavy bumblebees moving around the flower cups in their uncertain-certain way unerringly finding nectar and if you look, trying to understand by looking, that we are the temporary interlopers that they as much as possible work around and ignore, and if you close your eyes and try to hold the vision of the sunlight and the way it fills and illuminates the space of the garden, and if you just hold it there to its vanishing point when the vision itself dissembles into a remembered and glowing light a throbbing candescence . . . You, Regina, your paintings taught me this.

I rambled on and as I did so, I opened my eyes, and there next to me Regina sat with her eyes closed and I waited for her to open her eyes, and when she opened her eyes she told me that she never stopped being a painter of light.

D o you know, Gideon, Regina said to me, I never finished up my diploma at the University of Chicago. All my friends had graduated class of 1988 except for me. I had gone through some hard times just after we knew each other. I didn't know what I wanted to do with my life. I had thrown myself into painting on a whim. I had taken a studio painting class my second year at the college and I started painting obsessively on large canvases investigating the expressive properties of yellow and white and ocher and orange and red and purple paints and I too was chasing after something with my painting, I was chasing after an inner vision that centered itself on a range of colors not unrelated to what I call the revelation of the morning or evening sun, as the sun either emerges from the horizon line flooding the zone with light or sinks beneath the horizon line thereby draining the zone of light, and at first, my art professor, Gwendolyn Davis, whose career as an artist was founded not upon painting but upon art installations that rethought the formal innovations of Duchamp expanding the range of an object's meaning within the context of the space within which the object was shown, but Gwendolyn Davis's contribution was to rethink the meaning of the space, what she called the "metonym of the art object." What Gwendolyn Davis liked to talk about was the space. She would say things like: If the space (a gallery or an art museum) within which an art object was presented named the properties of the object and yet if the object presented within the space that was naming its properties was not also able to have a correlative effect on the space, then an art object's meaning only existed in the bell jar of the space; but she, Gwendolyn Davis, in her own art practice attempted to use art objects in ways that subverted and changed the meanings of the space they were exhibited in, thereby attempting to break the so-called bell jar that they were represented in. Gwendolyn Davis, Regina went on to say to me, always used to say, "Be aware of the bell jar"; or "Kung fu the bell jar"; or "Explode the bell jar"; or, "Contemporary art is just a bunch of hot houseplants inside a bell jar but the bell jar must be exploded."

My interior vision which I was struggling to make manifest in my paintings while I was in her class was meaningful to her because that vision was founded as much in the interior space of my own imagining as it was from light that I was attempting to capture in the real world. She, Gwendolyn Davis, encouraged me to find ways to blend both the interior light which I was attempting to record with the exterior light that I was also attempting to record, and as I worked in her class, she took me under her wing as if I were or as if I might be a prodigy worthy of her special attention, but her special attention was also a distraction because I was shy and because in its own way it was a perturbation upon my own vision and upon my own way of seeing. Nonetheless, her telling me that I was a painter of both sunrises and sunsets both as I saw them in my mind's eye and as I saw them in the world, and what's more, her telling me that I was talented at painting sunrises and sunsets, set me on a path of painting rather obsessively sunrises and sunsets and I had painted so many pictures of the sun emerging from below the horizon line which in this case, as I lived, at the time, in Hyde Park on the South Side of Chicago, it was naturally the sunrise as it rose in all of its daily splendor above Lake Michigan that I painted, or it was the sunset as our daily star sank beneath the horizon line to the west, I don't know, what is straight west of here or of Hyde Park? But my teacher's comments that I was gifted, or as she put it "talented" at painting the emergence or the disappearance of our daily star, the sun, had focused my attention on what I should do as a painter, and I did it. I painted with extreme focus. I tried to speak my talent, if you will. I know this might all sound so stupid and foolish to you. You, after all, have written that book of yours, Gideon, your so-called confession, but this thing I was doing painting the sun as it sat askance to the horizon line, it consumed me and it continued to consume me until I saw, I kid you not, the paintings of that painter, Thomas Kinkade, but it wasn't until I saw, quite by accident, I was reading a magazine in a hair salon while I waited for my hairdresser, and I was reading one of the magazines they have at the hair salon, and I saw an article on the painter of light, Thomas Kinkade, but it wasn't until I had read that article when I realized that as long as all I did was follow my talent, which was to paint, as my teacher, Gwendolyn Davis, had told me to do, sunrises and sunsets, that even if I pursued this art with monogamous zeal, with the dedication of a saint, that I would never come close to approaching the paintings of Thomas Kinkade and that as a painter all I could do was follow him. When I realized that against the magnificent work of Thomas Kinkade, who already had mastered the art of the sunrise and sunset, and the direction that he had charted for painters of light into the mall gallery, that all I would ever be, if, in fact I were ever to be any good at what I did, was a second fiddle, at best I would even be a second fiddle to Thomas Kinkade and if I was lucky, I would follow him into the mall gallery. When I had this realization, what I call my "fateful" realization, I immediately gave up painting. I couldn't think of anything more futile than to become Thomas Kinkade's second fiddle. And so I was bereft. I was searching for something else to replace my painting, which I had sworn to give up, but I was searching for that other thing that would replace painting in my life. It was then, while I was still occupying that studio that my dad had purchased for me, when I ran into you.

At the time, you and my best friend, Claire, were just starting to date, but for whatever reason, you and I had "caught eyes" as they say, and not long after that you had made your way to my studio, and that's when, letting you into my studio, showing you some of my paintings that I had done, and watching your reaction to my paintings, you looked at me in a way that no one before or since has ever looked at me, though, since the publication of your book, where you portrayed for the world to see, the intimate sexual encounter that you and I had shared, there have been others who have read your book, and then looked me up and have solicited from me a sexual encounter that would repeat for them the sexual encounter that you and I had had, a sexual encounter, by the way, that I never thought I would have in the first place, and I certainly never thought that having a sexual encounter with you, who, by the way, was just starting to date my best friend, but I never thought that my sexual encounter with you would make its way back in gossip and innuendo to Claire, which, in fact it did, and this caused me to have to confront Claire with the truth thereby ending my friendship with Claire, but I thought it even less likely that this encounter that you and I had would find its way into a book that you, Gideon, of all people had written and why did I think that our sex would never make it into a book? Because at the time you and I had had sex, you weren't even a writer for god's sake! And for two, I never thought that what you and I had done between ourselves was worth remembering, or gossiping about to Claire, or even memorializing in your book. But the truth is, Gideon, we had sex after you saw my paintings, and I was amazed that my paintings had such an erotic effect on you, and furthermore, I actually did like the sex we had. But the next morning, I swore you off, and I promise I will never have you again as long as I live, not just because I wouldn't want it to show up in another book, should you write one, but because I want to hold true to that instinct I had of you the morning after we had had sex in my studio. My instinct was to let a fox be a fox but to let that fox be a fox in some other person's henhouse, not mine.

All that being said, I had given up painting because I never wanted to be a second fiddle to Thomas Kinkade nor did I want my paintings to follow his into the mall gallery business, but in your book you describe seeing something different than what my teacher saw: you saw me as a kindred spirit of Turner. I too had seen Turner's paintings at the Tate, and, after reading your description of my work, which at the time were the truest words ever written of my work, I began to see a new path forward for my work. I sold the studio my father had purchased for me. I bought a loft space on the Chicago River near Chinatown, and I started a new career chasing after an image that you sketched out for me in your book, and for that, Gideon, for helping to jump-start my career with your book, I owe you the deepest debt of gratitude.

Anyway, what I wanted to say, Gideon, because you got me thinking, but here's the thing. That day when you came to my studio, I remember that you stood in the middle of the studio and light flooded the studio, and my canvases hung on the walls, and at the time I had been broken by the realization that I couldn't fulfill my vision as well as I might and I was deeply concerned that I would always be second fiddle, that is if I were as great as my talent suggested I might be, because hard work and talent can take you only so far, but other people's talent and hard work might take them even further, and I wasn't capable of going as far out as Thomas Kinkade and when I realized that, I decided I should devote my energies to something other than painting, but that's when you came into my studio, Gideon, and at first it seemed you had a passion for seeing me, but it wasn't until you saw my artwork hanging on the wall, when suddenly I saw that who I was as a person and what I might be to you, Gideon, that very moment didn't matter, what mattered more than anything to you at that moment was the erotic effect of my paintings on you. I could see their effect on you. I could see the effect of my paintings working on you, and I had never seen my paintings have an erotic effect quite like they did on you, Gideon. I saw that my paintings had the power to divert your eye from me, because I know that ever since we saw each other that first time in the restaurant when Claire introduced me to you as her "best friend in all the world," I knew even as she introduced me to you that when you saw me you were filled with lust for me and it was a decision that you put to me when we first saw each other, whether I would let you satisfy that lust for me or whether I would make you pine for me. Somehow, though, and I don't know how, maybe Claire told you where my studio was, maybe I told you where my studio was, but you made your way in the rain to my studio and knocked on the door of my studio, I let you in, and you were wet in your clothes from the rain, and there was lust, and at that moment, the rain had stopped and light started to flow into my studio again because the clouds overhead had parted, and the paintings, that I had lived with for so long I had forgotten all about them, but the paintings were there on the wall, and that's when you, Gideon, turned from me to the paintings and it was as if you forgot not only who I was, this stranger that you were lusting over, but as if you forgot yourself or at least forgot your lust. You just stood there in the center of my studio looking at my paintings and you did that thing with your eyes. You stared at my canvases and then you closed your eyes and then you stared some more at my canvases then you closed your eyes as if in meditation, and I see that even now you have that habit of looking at things like the garden outside this window with the blooming magnolia tree, but you see things, the light, as you say, and you try to retain the light by closing your eyes.

And I saw you do that that day at my studio, and though you described the lump in your throat that my paintings had caused you to have, I saw something else. I saw the lump in your pants. I saw that whatever lust and erotic attraction you, Gideon, may have had for me was transferred to a lust and an almost erotic attraction for my canvases. I saw, with my own eyes, the almost physiological effect that my paintings had on you. It's as if my paintings somehow found the inner switch that turned on the light in the small darkroom of your soul and that light produced pleasure. I saw . . .

It was the brushstrokes, I told her. It was the light that you were able to render out of paint on your canvases but it was also your brushstrokes.

Yes. That's what you told me that day, Gideon, and you didn't write that in your book. You told me that my brush-strokes were the sexiest most sensual brushstrokes that you had ever seen a painter make on a canvas, and that idea, that maybe I wasn't simply a painter of light, like Thomas Kinkade or Turner, but that I was a painter of sensuous brushstrokes that might cause a lustful reaction in the viewer, this is what you taught me that day when you visited me in my studio. You came to my studio to have an illicit fuckfest with me while you were also trying to date my friend Claire, but then you saw my paintings and you wanted somehow or another to fuck them, but because you couldn't fuck them, then you came and fucked me while thinking all the while neither of me nor Claire but of the sensuous beauty of the brushstrokes, markings on a canvas that I had made. Remember, Gideon, that you wrote this of me in your famous book . . .

"She was fat, with a big round ass. Tattoos of names and numbers—algebra, calculus, a shibboleth of numeric data that added up to some algorithm with runic import—proliferated in inky darkness across the canvas of her body . . ."

Do you remember writing that in your book about me, Gideon? Do you remember writing those words? Because I haven't forgotten the words. They are profane and vulgar and explicit. They represent a stealing, a theft. You purloined me for public scrutiny.

I don't remember writing those words, Regina, I confessed, nor do I remember thinking it, but if you say I wrote it, and it does sound like something that I might have written, then I apologize for revealing details about your personhood that should have remained private to you and I should not have shared those details to the world, but you'll have to remember, Regina, I still don't know why I wrote that book, nor did I anticipate at the time I published the book the wild reception that it would get in the world . . .

I remember it, Regina said, how could I not. Word for word. It's partly what has made me famous. Regina laughed, suddenly. She put her hand over her mouth to keep any particles of food from flying out of her mouth, then she looked at me both accusingly and with pain in her eyes.

Even though I laugh, you are absolutely not forgiven, Gideon, Regina said. And I will try to make you pay for that private description of me, that portrait, so to speak, that you had penned of my naked body. Those so-called runic symbols belong to me: they are my interiority made external upon a skin not to be revealed but in the most intimate moments and once revealed they were not to be shared beyond the intimate moment we shared. They are a speaking, my so-called runic symbols, that do not speak but hide, rather, behind the inscrutable silence of their own runes. Maybe one day I will speak that silence to you, Gideon, until then I won't forgive you for what you revealed of my secret signs in your oh-so-public book. But what the words in your book failed to say was that thing you told me when you first saw and were captivated by the paintings in my studio: that the brushstrokes on my canvas were the most sensuous and beautiful brushstrokes that you had ever seen painted on a canvas. I sometimes wonder why of all the privacies you divulged in that memoir of yours that there were these additional and what I think might be even more private privacies that you failed to disclose and what, had you disclosed them, might have made your memoir an even more truthful book. But you told me that about my sensuous brushstrokes and by failing to disclose that observation in your book it became essentially a secret that you and I shared and whether or not you remembered what you told me when you first saw my paintings, and maybe you forgot what you told me and that's why it never appeared in your memoir, but I remembered, Gideon, and that day, your reactions to my paintings, you woke me up to the idea that I could pursue my art passion, which at that point I had vowed to give up, in fact I was in the process of trying to divest myself of the studio that my father had purchased for me on Sixty-First Street and Dorchester, but I had vowed to divest myself of this ambition to pursue my talent to paint pictures because even though I had the talent to paint sunrises and sunsets I realized I would never be even nearly as good as Thomas Kinkade, but your observations freed me from the burden of competing with Thomas Kinkade. You revealed to me that my true talent might be to make brush-strokes on the canvas and that maybe the secret power that I as a painter possessed was to paint brushstrokes that were so naturally sensuous and as you say "sexy" that they made the viewer quite literally want to fuck the canvas. And that's what I have set out to do these last seventeen years, and I've shifted the burden of lust that people might have had for me to the canvas and that has liberated me from the gaze of others, but I have seduced the gaze nevertheless, like a bullfighter seduces the bull with the cape. Though rather than with a sword, the bullfighter's *espada*, I seduce and kill with paintbrush in hand following a ritualized set of gestures that allow me to get at the most private of privacies.

And how did you do this, Regina? I asked her. How did you come to do this, what was your method of discovery other than what you impute you discovered that afternoon seventeen years ago, when I had stepped into your studio?

I didn't know exactly how I would go forward but that afternoon after our tryst which you memorialized in your book, Gideon, I knew that I would go forward into my life as a painter. It was as if your gaze on my painting had not only liberated me from the male gaze, transferring it instead to my canvas, but it's as if your gaze had also liberated me from trying to compete with painters of light and primarily as I construed my main competition to be, Thomas Kinkade, and more distantly by inspiration only to the late paintings of Turner at the Tate, whose lineal antecedence to my work you, Gideon, to your credit, correctly identified and that is why I took your observation of my brushstrokes to heart and so though I knew that I would still be a painter of light I came to understand that ultimately I would become primarily a painter of brushstrokes. That afternoon, seventeen years ago, when you left my studio, Gideon, I made two decisions, first: I decided that I would go through with my plan to sell the studio that my father had purchased for me, and second: I decided I would tell my father that rather than giving up painting, I had changed my mind, and I would like to continue to make a go of it. To that end, we sold my studio, and with the money and a bit of extra money from my father I purchased a two-story loft studio on the Chicago River near the St. Charles Air Line Bridge at Sixteenth Street, which was a perfect location for me because I intended to move forward with my painting career only I wanted to find a new place to conduct my work that was far enough away from the gravitational pull of the University of Chicago that I wouldn't be overly influenced by daily interactions with my former teachers there, and particularly I needed to situate myself far enough away from Gwendolyn Davis that she could still inform me in my own art practice, but that she wouldn't usurp my practice which I was still in the process of trying to work out. I sought a separate space where I could work in solitude and find my own path forward and that's what the Chinatown location has given me. When I moved there, the light in that studio it is so beautiful and inspirational, Gideon, it's almost otherworldly in its luminous properties but I began painting again following along the pathways that I had started on at the University of Chicago. I continued to paint the balancing of the sun, trying to capture through a range of warm and cool colors that light I was actually experiencing in my studio on Sixteenth Street and as the late Turners in the Tate veered toward a sort of premodern abstract expressionism of sunlit clouds, I began from that spot, in my own artwork, where Turner had left off, and I began replicating as much as I could replicate, the manner of his paintings, and by replicating those painting several centuries hence with the materiality of contemporary paint resources and painting in the dawn of my own modernity and from the locale of my new studio the replications took on necessarily my own vernacularism; a female vernacularism, if you will, of our own contemporary moment and as I painted my canvases which were large-scale nine-foot-by-nine-foot square canvases I let my brushstrokes become what you, Gideon, indicated they were, sensuous, almost melodiously beautiful brushstrokes and it took a while before I was confident enough to fill a whole canvas with brushstrokes that subtly smeared the paint in a provocative way but I too, like you, Gideon, with your eyes shut contemplating the garden, followed my brush in my own contemplation of things as it stroked the canvas and in that place where the paint touches the canvas I try to find the bliss of my own eternity and it's in trying to find both the bliss and the eternity, the joining place of those two things where I make my art, and over time as I became more confident with my art, I found that the armature of the Turner imagery slowly fell away until all that was left was paint on a canvas and not wanting to distract from the brushstrokes with color or imagery I moved toward making white and black diptych paintings and burying portraits in the paint that only the brushstrokes disclose, but more importantly I attempt in each of my diptychs on the one hand with the white painting to portray the womblike interiority of a cloud just at its moment of maximum brightness and on the other hand with the black painting to recover the vibration of light on the retina of the closed eye caused by the brightness of the light found in the white painting and I've been making these buried portraits and diptych paintings where the sensuality and sexiness of my brushstrokes that you noted and the bliss of eternity somehow get all mixed up, but I've been making my own peculiar form of minimalism consistently for over a decade. Of course, I have you, Gideon, to thank not only for mentioning me in your book, but for mentioning my paintings on *The Oprah Winfrey Show* because that mention, more than anything else, has launched my career as the successful painter that I am today.

Did showing your paintings in the Whitney Biennial, as Claire informed me you had done, make you happy, Regina?

I couldn't believe it was happening to me of all people, if that's what you want to know, Regina said to me, the fame thing wasn't something I sought, rather it feels more like fame sought me out and when I saw my paintings hanging in the Whitney Biennial and when later I had seen the crowds at the show flock around my paintings, and when my paintings as a result started to sell for ridiculous sums, and then there was the Guggenheim Fellowship, followed by the MacArthur award . . . all of these accolades for my paintings, I don't know how to reconcile all of this with my own sense of self, which, I must confess, I am a solitary creature who spends all day painting, and like I say, I felt more hunted down by the fame machine and captured by it like some animal in a trap, and ever since I have retreated more aggressively into the bunker of my studio. But you too, Gideon, have had some accolades as a result of your famous book. So maybe you know what I'm talking about . . .

As to the fame of my book and the fame of your artwork, Regina, I told her, what was a bewildering experience for you—your fame and your success as an artist— has been for me, also a solitary person prone to retreat into my own world, actually a catastrophizing experience . . .

I felt the bile build up in me whenever I found myself talking about this part of my life and when the bile started to become unbearable, I learned how to make it slightly more bearable just by laughing, and so I started laughing and Regina started laughing and while she sat across from me in the coffee shop I could swear not a moment had transpired since the last time I saw her even though in point of fact seventeen years had passed since I last saw her and I told her so: Other than remembering the beauty of your paintings, Regina, which I confess that I have done everything in my powers to forget as I have tried to forget everything else from the past that is my life, and who knows, maybe writing that stupid book, *Gideon's Confession*, which I regret not only having written, but in some ways I felt duped by my publisher into having published, duped because he said that the manuscript that I had sent him absolutely must be published, and I don't know why I fell under his sway because I was not invested at all in what I had written, and I still don't know why I had sent the publisher the manuscript in the first place, other than I had been at a party and I was sitting next to a writer, an old Kentucky gentleman, who has since become, I kid you not, partly famous for launching me as a writer, but I was sitting at a party next to this Kentucky gentleman, who had just published a book about his boyhood in Kentucky that was a combination shoeless-country-boy book, a University of Pennsylvania coming-of-age story to where he had matriculated, miraculously from his impoverished beginnings, and then on to Harvard Law School where he studied and then made a career for himself in international criminal law and practiced at The Hague for thirty years where he had helped prosecute war crimes of Khmer Rouge leaders involved in the Cambodian genocide, but I had been sitting next to this elderly Kentucky gentleman, who still spoke with the vestigial vocalizations of his Kentucky upbringing, but sitting next to him and in a moment of weakness, I divulged to him that I too had written a memoir of sorts, and after I described the book to him, he introduced me to his agent, who as it happens was also sitting at the table with us that evening, and after drinking several bottles of wine and glasses of bourbon I was encouraged to send my manuscript to this Kentucky gentleman's agent, which I did, hungover and not thinking correctly, next morning, and within days, caught up in the swoon and enthusiasm of the Kentucky gentleman's agent, who had read my book in its entirety as soon as he received it and who followed up with me immediately notifying me that the book, which at the time was titled *The Ark of Disquiet*, must absolutely be published because the marketplace at the time hadn't seen a book like mine from a member of my generation, what he called "your generation," but a member of my generation had yet to write a memoir wherein a confession was made, and he, the agent, referred to it as quite possibly a "generational confession," wherein I disclosed that despite the generous monthly checks my uncle had sent me to underwrite my day-to-day life, and despite every advantage conferred upon me by my education at the University of Chicago, and even more, in light of the driven—"your driven"—father, the agent had said, and of the driven nature of your brothers who also aspired to be as driven as your driven father, but despite all of these advantages, you, Gideon, my prospective agent told me, preferred to swim, like a goldfish, in the very small fishbowl that had become your life, which was a renunciation, and he, the agent, put it this way, "your renunciation of a capitalistic way of life." You weren't, strictly speaking, a loafer or a slacker, and he used that word, "slacker," which at the time he used it was still not part of common parlance, instead the agent had said, Your memoir speaks by allusion and through your depiction of your day-to-day life, of the emergence, of what I can only call "the indolence gene," and this agent, who after reading my manuscript asked to become my agent, wondered aloud in our telephone conversation, if my book signaled the arrival of a new generational gestalt, was this to become "the Slacker Generation," the generation that had been poisoned off the mad scramble for cash and fame, the generation born not with the ambition gene but with the, and he used this phrase, the "indolence gene." Thank god, he said to me on the telephone call, that you weren't so indolent that you failed in your indolence to pen your manuscript, but this manuscript, I have great confidence in it, I do believe it may become a generation-defining book, and with that he requested permission to send my manuscript to an editor friend of his at Noname Press, which, for reasons I still don't understand, because, here's the thing, Regina, I had written a private record of my final year at the University of Chicago, and what had compelled me to write that manuscript? And I've since come to think that the reason why I had written that manuscript of my final year at the University of Chicago was because I desperately wanted to forget and put behind me everyone and everything that I had done that year. I wanted to forget you, Regina, and Claire and everyone else I knew back then. I wanted to forget my uncle who wrote those monthly checks. I wanted to forget his wife, Nan, who in turn desperately wanted to forget me. She too used that word, "slacker," whenever she had the chance to insult me in front of my uncle. I wanted to forget the bar and all my friends at the bar. I wanted to forget my life. I wanted to let go. I wanted to be purged, and to be honest, at the time, I didn't understand why I had wanted to purge myself of a year of lived experience and of all the connections that I had made that year, other than for this simple reason: that year, those experiences, and those human connections had filled me with bile, with disgust and revulsion, and I had wanted to puke, literally vomit, the entire year out of my system and I didn't know how to do that, but I had discovered quite randomly that by writing of that year in a small diary, and then typing that diary onto an early Apple computer, I felt as if I had found a way to make the "emptying" happen. Writing seemed to empty me of the anxiety and disgust that remembrance of that year had filled me with, and so, with an eye to try and heal myself of all the disgust that that year had filled me with, I trod on with my daily typing in order to purge myself. I had unloaded all the animals of my discontent onto the ark of that manuscript, *The Ark of Disquiet*, and the idea started to emerge that once I had filled the manuscript with all the things that had filled me with loathing that year of my final year at the University of Chicago, then I would take my manuscript, print it up, then I'd delete the file from my floppy disk, and on a windy day I would go to the rocks of Promontory Point and release my manuscript's pages into the stormy waters of Lake Michigan, and in this way, with a "flushing of the toilet," so to speak, purging myself of the shit and bile that had filled me to the brim, and cleansed of my past, I could then proceed into the world to start again, becoming in the process a new me.

A new Gideon, Regina exclaimed.

Yes. A new me. That was the goal of the whole project: to write the book, filling it like Noah's ark with all the creaturely memories that filled me with bile, and once these memories were transferred to that ark, then on a stormy day I would delete the file and release that ark upon the waters of Lake Michigan, thereby flushing away the great turd of a manuscript . . . Only, what happened instead, is that I had run into that Kentucky gentleman, whose grandson's book I have right now in my hand, and which I was reading, a book his grandson has provisionally titled *man/dog/cure*, which I think is a very good title, and which I am in the process of blurbing as a favor to the old Kentucky gentleman, but it was my having met in the first place the Kentucky gentleman, and in a moment of weakness I had explained to the Kentucky gentleman the nature of the manuscript I had just written, and I think I had even mentioned, though I'm not sure, that I was waiting for the weather to turn malign so that in the cataract that storming Lake Michigan could become, I would release my manuscript like a turd upon its waters and I would be purged of everything that I had loaded into that manuscript and I would begin to start a new day as a new me and it was at this moment, the moment when I said the words, "my manuscript turd," when the Kentucky gentleman introduced me to his agent, who then read my manuscript and passed it along to a friend of his, an editor at Noname Press, and by the end of the week, faster than I thought things like this could happen, I was offered a substantial advance in lieu of Noname Press's right to publish my book, and since the advance was significant enough to allow me to carry on doing nothing in the way that my deceased uncle's checks had allowed me to carry on doing nothing during that final year at the University of Chicago, I could not say no, and so that's how my book came to be published, and my agent was not incorrect in his initial appraisal of my book, because after publication of the book, and the small stir that it had created, an emergent theme came to describe a portion of our generation, we became Generation Slacker, and my book, *Gideon's Confession*, was exhibit A as evidence for this generational change.

In any event, publication of the book, which I dreaded, did not purge me of my disquiet as I thought tossing my manuscript into Lake Michigan might have purged me. In fact, to become the emergent epicenter of Generation Slacker was tantamount to becoming my generation's turd. I was spinning in the toilet bowl of the whirling publicity machine that had gathered around my book with centrifugal forces and just when I hoped that me and my book might be flushed down the drain and disappeared for good, the daytime talkshow hosts and the publicists at Noname Press arranged that I would do interviews on television and radio for which I thought myself ill-equipped, even though those same television marketers and book publicists judged that I, to the contrary, was a potentially telegenic and a congenially humorous interview subject. I had a knack for speaking incisively about any and all things of little to no merit, a talent developed during my years spewing bullshit at the bar with my regular group of cronies. I also had a natural inbuilt "anomie"; I had a general chip on my shoulder that was big as a granite boulder. It was thought by said publicists that all of these characteristics that I possessed might pay off on the publicity circuit and books might be sold en masse. If you say you hate success, they're going to love it, I heard one marketer advise me.

I said over and over again in those interviews that I should have never written the book, and having written the book I should have done what I had originally intended to do, I should have marched it over to Promontory Point and tossed it, like Noah's ark, onto the waters of Lake Michigan to be lost forever, but instead, like a fool, I had allowed myself to be talked into publishing the book—and this, for me, was what I hated. This was the beginning of my disaster.

I told the story about how even though my agent was

bullish on the book, my editor had taken a more equanimous position saying it could go either way: in other words publication of the book could be a flop or it could be a smash hit. My publicist, on the other hand, judged the temperament of the zeitgeist correctly. He thought not only that the negative energy in my book was a hallmark of my generation, your generation, he said, but that this negative energy could in turn be used to sell the book. In any event, it was a long shot, he said, that the book would succeed, but it had prospects. He alluded to the enthusiasm of my agent, and he even hearkened to the smaller yet significant enthusiasm of the old Kentucky gentleman, and he said they liked it, meaning my agent and the old Kentucky gentleman, and they know a thing or two about books, so who knows, anything can happen.

In fact, as we came to discover, not a month after *Gideon's Confession* was published the book hit the top of the *New York Times* best-seller list, and after that the name "the Slacker Generation" had become so closely associated with my book that my life as I knew it was turned upside down. I went from anonymous to famous, and since then, I've never been able to go back to normal.

That's when all the people in the world who had ever had a kind thought for me gave me up as an asshole, and all the unknown and myriad assholes of the world started to reach out to me as their spokesman, "our spokesman" they would call me, that is if they weren't calling me King Slacker or the Slacker King.

You, Regina, were alive when my book was published. You saw the dog and pony show on *The Oprah Winfrey Show* or at least I assume you did, because how could you have missed it? It has become one of her most watched segments, but it was on that segment where she too referred to me as the new spokesman of Generation Slacker and she, Oprah, even referred to me with a little mirth as King Slacker, yet before the show was filmed do you know, Regina, she, Oprah, invited me to have lunch with her in her studio office at Harpo Studios and she, Oprah, told me when just she and I were sitting together that my brand-new book had meant something to her. I see all sorts of books, Gideon, Oprah said. I earn my money pitching books. But your book, Gideon, I would have pitched it for free. That's how much it meant to me.

Well, it doesn't mean anything to me, I told Oprah Winfrey that afternoon. We were eating shrimp scampi in the privacy of her office and she, Oprah, was really quite approachable. It was amazing to me just how approachable Oprah was backstage, just the two of us eating our lunch in the privacy of her office. I felt I was sitting across from just another person, and the scale of her, Oprah's, personhood as colossal as it is on the world stage, but in the antechamber of her studio she had managed to shrink herself down to normal proportions, and I, Gideon, was able to see eye to eye with her, Oprah, person to person rather than as person to the colossus that she most definitely is, and this opportunity I had to see Oprah as a person with whom I might relate, and let's not forget, there's no little truth in the description of my book as it being a book for the Slacker Generation, and in fact, the book featured me as a poster boy of slackerdom, so to be who I was, which was essentially an unknown nobody who sought nothing from the world other than a sort of plain subsistence-style life, subsidized no doubt in part and sometimes in whole by my uncle, but to be this absolute nobody and by the publication of my book, and the vagaries of timing as such things as books might hit the zeitgeist of the moment, but by virtue of this zeitgeist I had first scaled to the top of the *New York Times* best-seller list, which in itself is ludicrous to consider, but then, by virtue of my scaling the heights of the *New York Times* best-seller list my publicist had all the information he needed, stellar reviews pointing to my book as "the voice piece of a new generation; shall we call it Generation Slacker?" a writer for the *New Yorker* had written, and with these reviews in hand a deal was cut, a startling and surprising deal that I, Gideon, appear on Oprah Winfrey's show as part of her book club series, and so, having agreed to show up on her show, I found myself quite by surprise alone in a room with Oprah, and it was here where I confronted her utter humanity, her sense of humor, her amazing beauty, it was breathtaking to behold and who was I to deserve this sudden audience with Oprah, but an idiot that's all I really was, a pranking idiot, an utter jackass, who had penned a stupid memoir as an afterthought to a period of time, my final year at the University of Chicago that for inexplicable reasons I completely wanted to forget. So there I was when she was telling me about why she thought my book was so authentic and meaningful and as she, Oprah, said this I poked a shrimp with my fork and swirled it with a bit of pasta into the butter sauce and I stuffed it all into my mouth trying hard not to get any of the butter sauce onto my brand-new navy blazer which I had purchased with the remnant stash of my uncle's money at the discount clothier, Men's Warhorse, and which I hoped might make me look presentable for the duration of whatever trials and tribulations by fire and post that might plague me on the long and wearying rounds of publicity that I was now obliged to make thanks to the unwelcome and unexpected and ridiculous success of my book, and I told Oprah how writing the book was the most forgettable exercise that I had ever committed myself to and just the idea that people were calling me a writer, and hailing me as my generation's spokesman, or spokesperson, that I was called the Slacker King, it was all such a terrible embarrassment to me, and do you know, I told Oprah, that had my uncle lived to see that I had written about him and talked about the checks that he had signed for me during the last few years that he was alive, if he had been alive to see the mistake that I had made writing about his generosity, and then publishing it as a book, well, he would be ashamed of me, and I told all this to Oprah Winfrey while we had lunch in her studio before filming our interview at Harpo Studios, and she listened as beautifully as she naturally listens, and she said to me, Oprah said to me, Gideon, I suppose that your desire not to have written the book, and your even deeper desire not to have published the book, but I bet it was these twin desires that made your book the authentic masterpiece, and she used that word, "masterpiece," and I almost choked on my shrimp scampi as I consider the absurdity of the situation I had gotten myself into . . . the authentic masterpiece, Oprah continued, that your book is and she started to tell me how my book reminded her of herself, of her deepest self, and while we ate lunch together alone in her office, she revealed to me that her dearest self was the self that no one had ever encountered, it was a self that had long ago disappeared under the carapace of fame. Too many eyes have seen and watched me, too many minds have contemplated my every move, too many tongues have spoken of me and what they have collectively concluded is something that is not spoken so much as felt, Oprah told me while we were eating shrimp scampi, just she and I, an hour or so before we were to be filmed together on her show, And what is felt by the collective is a sort of awe that they have of me, an awe wherein they seem to be perpetually holding their breath as if they cannot believe what they see before their very eyes, that a woman like me, Oprah Winfrey, that a Black woman, can not only command the world's attention, but that I can cast a spell upon all those who look upon me. I'm not a witch, and I don't have any malign motivations, though what I am primarily is an actor, a Black woman, and a TV talk show host whose special power is listening. I don't know how I learned to listen, Gideon, Oprah told me, though I can tell you, and I think you will understand because I have read your book, *Gideon's Confession*, and so I think I know something about you, but my ability to listen, which is an ability some people think that I must have been born with, but here's the thing, Oprah told me, I told Regina that morning while we talked in the coffee shop, I was a solitary child, Oprah said, who was loved by my mother and though I did have friends and though I had family, nevertheless I was primarily a solitary, almost a lonely child, and it was from this childhood that I learned how to turn my ear to the world, so to speak, and listen. It was a natural talent of mine. I knew how to ask questions and how to follow up with more questions, but all of my questions were predicated on the fundamental act of listening and while I followed where my gift, if you will, of listening would take me, nevertheless there was always that little girl, solitary, beloved child of my mother, who lurks within this carapace of fame that I have become and that child who lurks within me wishes that rather than being locked up in the famous brand that Oprah Winfrey has become that she might be freed, hatched from the chrysalis, reborn anew from the carapace and shell of this famous person, and that's why, Oprah told me as I finished my shrimp scampi, your book speaks to me, because your book addresses not Oprah Winfrey who you will meet very shortly upon our studio stage, but oprah, little oprah, the oprah that no one knows about: the oprah who cares nothing about any of this, and she waved her fork to indicate the world that Harpo Studios had created, your book spoke to that little girl, oprah, and for that I am thankful. I thanked Oprah for the intimacy that she had shared with me and then moments later we were on her show. I wasn't prepared for the show or for Oprah Winfrey proper. You'll remember, I told Regina, that even at this moment Oprah was one of the biggest personalities in the world, and she had become famous for her book club and for all of the famous writers and not-so-famous writers who, because they were invited onto her show had become, by virtue of that invitation, famous, and the same thing had happened to me, and at the time, I was naïve enough to think that I could appear on Oprah Winfrey's show and that I could go home afterward and not have fame happen to me, but something happened which I hadn't predicted and it was something my publicist hadn't prepared me for. I encountered, before a studio audience, not the Oprah Winfrey with whom I had had shrimp scampi just moments before in the privacy of her office, instead, I encountered the Oprah Winfrey on the studio stage with a live studio audience whom everyone knows and while I was onstage and while I was the focus of Oprah Winfrey's questions and while I became the focus of what I can only describe as Oprah's "ravenous" listening, I became aware of the fact that every word I uttered not only would become part of the public record, thereby defining me forever, but I also became aware of the fact that opposite me on a comfortable couch in a pleasant studio with a few hundred people in the audience was a presence so singular and focused and I don't know how else to say it, but she was a presence overladen with empathy, she was profound in her ability not just to listen but in her ability to comprehend me as if I were a being that she with her empathetic querying had come to embody, and so tell me, Oprah said, smiling at me in the most beautiful and loving and devastating way imaginable, and her utterance of the words "so tell me" was so filled with understanding and empathy, so embracing in its loving warmth, a warmth by the way that I had never encountered before, that when she said those words to me I thought I was going to instantly break down sobbing for all the world to see . . . so tell me, Oprah said to me in front of that studio audience, and then her face changed expression in a moment and she said, looking offstage at her producer, and then back to me, she said, Gideon, I wonder if you might do me a favor, I have never asked anyone on my show to dance with me, but we had such a warm conversation backstage before the show, and I wonder if you might do me the honor and do a brief little dance on the stage with me, do you know how to dance, Gideon, and I told Oprah that I knew how to do the two-step, and So do I, she said, and then a bit of music started up, and the chairs were moved to create room on the stage and Oprah came toward me with her arms reaching out to me and I reached for her hands, and in the shock of the moment I tried to be as elegant and honorable as possible and for a moment, a very brief moment, maybe only thirty seconds we danced swaying a two-step on her stage, and then the music quieted down, and she smiled at me and directed me to take a seat so that we could begin our interview, and without referencing the dance that we had just performed, though I still felt it in my body, and I still feel it to this day the slow gentle and lovely rhythm of swaying to the music, which I don't remember what music was played, some quiet waltz is how I remember it, a song without voice or lyric, an autumnal song, a sound of autumn leaves falling, though it wasn't that song "Autumn Leaves" as sung by Billie Holiday, but yet again, it might have been that song, what's important to me now is not that I've forgotten the song, but the intimacy of that shared space between Oprah's body and my body as we came together and drifted apart and came together again and the repetition of this movement once or twice and then it was over, but these movements, this sway, the movement of that intimate space between our bodies, it is one of the things that is so vivid in my memory that I swear there is not a day that goes by when I don't find myself swaying and when I realize I am still swaying with my now disappeared dance partner, Oprah Winfrey, I am struck yet again by the singular potency that Oprah as a human possesses and so we sit down after the brief two-step and I am still swaying and rocking as though adrift at sea and she asked me So how did you,

Gideon, come to write this marvelous memoir which, and I think that I told you this backstage, but which I would recommend to all of my viewers because unlike so many books that are published, unlike so many books that are worthy to be read because they are worthy books, there is something about your book, Gideon, that is different from all of these other books and it is that that I want to get at today in our interview, Gideon, and I think that the answer might be found, Oprah the actor and talk-show host said to me looking at me with the most profoundly direct gaze that has ever been settled on me, but I think, Oprah continued, that the answer for what makes your book so meaningful might be found in the causes and conditions of the book's composition, and I wonder if you, Gideon, could tell us a little about that, and it was the warmth that I felt coming at me from Oprah in an almost all-embracing and smothering hug of love that touched me as if it were indeed love that were coming from her, Oprah, to me, Gideon, and I was so unprepared for Oprah's love and honesty before that studio audience that I immediately choked up and started to weep, because prior to Oprah's love of me, I had never myself been the object of someone else's love and so because I had never been the object of love I had never felt it and never having felt it, I also had never been trained in how to become a fount of love that I might release upon another, in short I was neither a receiver nor a giver of love and I had gone through my whole life up until that moment I was onstage with Oprah, loveless, and it was that brief and should I say loving moment under the attention of Oprah Winfrey that had convinced me of this lack of love in my life, and this realization that I had been so deprived of love made me in turn well up with all sorts of unaccountable and uncontrollable emotions of grief and that's what in turn caused me to almost break down sobbing uncontrollably in front of Oprah and the live studio audience and all the world that was watching on their TV sets and there was a close-in focus of me and then a cut-to-commercial break while staff from the show came out from behind the curtains to work on me and bring me back to some sort of emotional stability so that the interview could continue and then the staff disappeared behind the curtains and the cameras blinked on and Oprah continued where she had left off. So we are back here with Gideon Anderson, whose book, *Gideon's Confession*, we are here to celebrate because it is a very special kind of book, a singular work written in an unforgettable voice, and Gideon, you and I were talking about what led you to write your fantastic memoir? I felt it again, Oprah's love, and I immediately wanted to love her back with all of my heart. I wanted to throw down my so-called coat as Sir Walter Raleigh had thrown his down upon the puddle to keep Queen Elizabeth's feet from getting wet and muddy, and like Sir Walter Raleigh I had felt a similar impulse to prostrate myself in a show of humility and gratitude before Oprah and so I tried to be as honest and direct as possible. I told Oprah that I had written the book because I had been my whole life unloved, and I had grown so weary of being unloved that I had wanted to purge myself of this weariness and the only way I could think to do that was to write this book. And then I went into a little bit of detail about my actual writing process. I told Oprah Winfrey in front of that live audience about how first I would write thoughts down in my diary and how my thoughts started to coalesce around events and people whom I had known my last year in college at the University of Chicago, and as these things coalesced on paper in my diary and I began to transcribe them into an early-model Apple computer with a goal that only became manifest to me as I proceeded with the project, and the goal as I envisioned it was to write down everything from that final year of college at the University of Chicago, to collect all the animals of my discontent, so to speak, as Noah had collected all of the animals prior to the flooding of the world and as he herded the animals upon his ark, so too had I herded the animals of my discontent into what was becoming a book that resembled a memoir of my final year at the University of Chicago, and the goal as I approached completion of that manuscript became increasingly clear to me: I would print up the manuscript in paper form, I would destroy the floppy disk that I had stored the manuscript on during its composition, and then on a foul Chicago afternoon when Lake Michigan was breaking against the rocks of Promontory Point, I would release the pages of my manuscript like a turd upon the waters of Lake Michigan thereby flushing myself of all the bile and disgust that had built up in me during those spring months at the University of Chicago and I told Oprah that in truth I never understood the meaning of Noah's ark. Why had God flooded the world to have only one witness to watch the flooding of the world; why did God need a witness and was it a torment and a torture to Noah himself to bear witness to the destruction of the world he had known, and though the story of Noah ends with the dove of peace and remembrance there was still the destruction of the world that he had known and so he too must have felt some bile and disgust of his own at God maybe, who had flooded and destroyed Noah's world that Noah wanted to purge himself of and though I didn't know in what manner Noah might have accomplished this purging, if he had even accomplished it at all, nevertheless, I too needed to purge myself not of what God had done to my world, but of what I felt of the world that was falling away into the past because like God I wanted to do something about my past, but rather than flooding it, which wasn't possible for me, I wanted to forget it entirely, which was the next best thing to flooding the world of my past, so I had printed my manuscript to release it upon the flood of Lake Michigan while it was in violent storm against the shoreline rocks, and while I waited for the clement weather to turn malign I was invited to a large dinner gathering where I sat next to a Kentucky gentleman and over the course of the meal he told me about his book, a memoir of chasing Khmer Rouge war criminals at The Hague and I told him about my manuscript which I wanted to flush like a turd into the waters of Lake Michigan, and just as I said these words he signaled to his agent who was also sitting at the table with us to tune in to our conversation and no sooner had I told the agent about the concept of my book than the agent asked me to send it to him, which I did and soon thereafter the agent had contacted me and asked permission to send it to a publisher and sooner than I thought things like this might be possible a sizable advance was sent to me to secure the publisher's right to publish my book, and before I knew it one thing led to another and that's how, quite honestly, I told Oprah that day, I had ended up on her show. This story received applause from the audience that was quite spontaneous and also quite loving, and Oprah Winfrey herself joined in the applause and as she clapped her hands with the audience she settled her loving attention on me and smiled at me with the most loving and approving smile I had ever seen and then we broke for another commercial break and before I knew it those folks re-emerged from behind the curtains; they touched up my face and wiped the perspiration from my brow, they asked me to gargle with Coca-Cola to free my vocal cords which were still constricted from the emotional "choking up" that had overcome me earlier in the show, they adjusted my mic, fixed my navy sport coat and we were on again, and this time as the audience clapped on cue, Oprah Winfrey continued the show by saying, Welcome back everyone, today we are talking to Gideon, otherwise known as "the Slacker King" or "King Slacker," or, I threw in, "the King of Slack," which garnered a laugh, and she started to dig into my book and why did I think that it had caused such a stir; Why, Gideon, Oprah Winfrey asked me, looking at me with love in her eyes, do you think your book has become the talismanic book of your generation? Why has it hit such a nerve? In fact, Oprah Winfrey went on, the *New York Times* has even called your "confession," and I'll read the review now, Oprah said, reading from a clipping of Michiko Kakutani's infamous *New York Times* review of my book, "In *Gideon's Confession* we hear the uncanny voice of a neglected generation that tells the story, in turn, of how it, this new, shall we give it a word, 'Slacker Generation' propagates its own forms of neglect and rebellion against capitalistic norms and shows that this 'Slacker Generation' prefers to sit out life in the local bar perfectly content to live off the generous welfare of wealthy benefactors but also willing without notice to bite the hand that feeds it. It is implicitly an unloved generation that can't decide whether or not it wants a hug." Oprah put the review aside and smiled at me above her glasses; "Bites the hand that feeds it," she repeated. The studio audience thus primed was suitably impressed, and in front of them I tried to lay down my coat as Sir Walter had laid his down before the queen. I tried to answer Oprah as honestly as possible; I told her I don't know why my book hit such a nerve, Oprah, and I'm surprised more than a little that it has touched a nerve, but now that I am sitting here talking to you about it, I am starting to realize that the book is about a man (me, Gideon) who was deprived of love and being deprived of love, it is also a story of how that man (me, Gideon) is unable to give love. And so it is a book written by a rejected young man who wanted to reject all those things that had rejected him and thus, I guess this, Oprah, is how you might explain the so-called biting of the hand that fed me, and then, I reiterated to Oprah and to her studio audience, that rather than getting the book published, which was never my intention, I had hoped instead to destroy the computer disk that the manuscript was saved on and print only one copy of the manuscript; I had intended to reject the book myself by tossing it into the waves of Lake Michigan during a storm with the hope of freeing myself of all the stories and their attendant emotions that had knotted up inside me, causing me to literally want to puke with nausea and disgust, and though I can't explain why I wanted to purge myself of a year of experiences and free myself of all the social bonds that had held me in place during that year, I nevertheless felt just that. I had felt a deep compulsion to rid myself of all this stuff and the tossing of my book upon the waves of Lake Michigan was my plan for how to get rid of it all, it was my way, writing the book then tossing it into the waters, that would help me flush myself in a cleansing moment of a year of lived experience, but rather than accomplishing all of this as I had intended, I wrote the book instead and published it and the rest, the book, all that the book may signify to those who read it, and all of this fame, the articles anointing my book as having something to do with slackerdom, these are now all things that I will need to figure out how to contend with because to be honest with you, Oprah, I never wanted any of this. I should have never written the book to begin with and having written it, I should have burned it, but instead I published it, and maybe all of these contradictory emotions and feelings of self-disgust are more common in my generation and that's why it touched a nerve. Though why anyone would want to call me a "slacker" and how people who read my book could construe my book as the anthem of the Slacker Generation, does such a thing even exist? But how anyone could read my book and conclude that it was some blueprint for a generation is beyond my ability to understand, because to be perfectly honest with you, Oprah, and with your studio audience, and with all of the folks tuning in today on their TVs, I don't know what my book is about other than it tells the story of a boy who grew up too fast, into a world that he somehow or other was never able to see himself playing an important or vital role in, and though you, Oprah, claim that my book has touched a nerve in you, even this escapes my comprehension, because you, unlike me, seem so very much at home in the world, while I feel bewildered and ousted, "wilded" is more the word, lost in the maze of my own wilderness and not able to find my way home.

There was more applause, this time on cue, and then Oprah promptly got off her chair and coming toward me she gestured that I should stand, which I did and then to my surprise she hugged me and I felt it instantly how this was the most profound and beautiful thing that would ever happen to me in my life, and then there was a break for commercial, and after the commercial break Oprah Winfrey started to focus in on some of the relationships that I described in the book and she touched on a little of what it was like to be a student at the University of Chicago, and then, quite suddenly she asked me to tell her and her studio audience a little more about the painter Regina Blast, who has figured out how to paint the light that we see when we die and go to heaven, and she asked me what those paintings actually looked like, and that's when, Regina, I tried to describe who you were; Regina Blast, I told the studio audience and Oprah Winfrey, is a tremendously talented painter, and of all the paintings that I had ever seen, and I pointed out that I was an avid visitor to the Art Institute of Chicago, but I sensed when I saw Regina's paintings, I told Oprah, that here was a brand-new talent discovering new ways to paint what I can only describe as a "light at the end of the tunnel" kind of light, the white light that you see when you die and your soul then progresses to heaven; her paintings, I told Oprah Winfrey, your paintings, I told Regina, were paintings that tried to convey holiness itself in all of its pure, blank glory. And after I had said this, Oprah Winfrey said, I'll have to look up Regina

Blast and maybe buy one of her paintings, then, while she's still early in her career and affordable. We broke again for commercial break. The Slacker King, ladies and gentlemen. Buy his book, *Gideon's Confession*, and read it. It's an important and moving book and it's one that has touched me very much. At commercial break more people came from behind the curtain. They removed my microphone and told me my stint with Oprah was finished and thank you very much, and thank you, I told them, and I looked over to Oprah Winfrey to thank her, but she was overtaken by her own set of people who had emerged from behind the curtains to primp her for the next segment of her show, but her segment with me was finished. I never had a chance to say thank you to Oprah nor did I ever have another word with her and within moments I was ushered out off the stage and then backstage where I collected my stuff and out the door of Harpo Studios I went where I caught a cab ride home and I thought that this was the end of it but in point of fact it was just the beginning because like I say, my body was still swaying to Oprah's, and I still felt deep in my bones the gentle swing and sway of her body.

G ideon, Regina said, smiling at me that morning in the coffee shop, your mention of my name and your description of my paintings on Oprah Winfrey's show changed my life. Do you know that? Oprah Winfrey actually visited me at my studio. The thing was, my studio had moved from Sixty-First Street and Dorchester to my new location, which has been my location for most of my career, so there was the whole problem of her showing up at my old studio, the original studio where you, Gideon, had first encountered my paintings, and after she discovered that I no longer inhabited the premises, she went on to discover where indeed I had moved. I often imagine the moment that Oprah, fresh off her interview with you, Gideon, and if I remember correctly, it was in the autumn, September, I remember it because the light that day was a September light with a shimmering frigid brightness though it was a warm day when she conducted her driver to my old studio on Sixty-First and Dorchester, which she was able to find because your description of my old studio in your book, *Gideon's Confession*, was so precise that it didn't need street corners for Oprah and her driver to ferret the place out, and when she rang the bell to my old studio, she discovered the current occupants of the place, a small group of social activists who wanted to use the space for local social change and this is what I imagine: the confusion the occupants of those premises felt and bewilderment not to mention their shock at seeing Oprah Winfrey outside their door with her driver demanding to know if there were still a young woman, Regina Blast, Oprah spoke my name out loud to them, an artist who used the premises to paint pictures, and why are you inquiring they might have asked the great lady, and she responding, because I am very curious to see the artwork of this woman I've been told paints light, a sort of "light at the end of the tunnel" kind of light, a "white light that you see when you die and go to heaven" kind of light, and I am so intrigued by the description of these paintings and by the type of light that these paintings are trying to represent that I'd like to visit her studio to see both her and her paintings, and having received such a response they, the occupants of my former studio who are social activists, might have given her the forwarding address I had left with them in case any mail from the post office had continued to trickle for me to that address. And it was only minutes later when driving up from the South Side they came to my studio on the north end of Chinatown and getting out of the dark SUV, the driver rang the bell to my studio and not anticipating having guests, and unused to visitors, I was startled by the bell to my studio, so much so that I leaped, causing my paintbrush to leave a mark of startlement on the canvas that I was working on, and looking out my window to see who it was, I was startled to see Oprah Winfrey standing outside my studio and her driver answering my bell by saying that Oprah Winfrey requests the privilege of visiting with me, and I buzzed her in immediately. Come please, I said, please come upstairs to the second floor, and up she came by herself, her driver stayed down by the car, and a moment later, in the space of my gallery stood Oprah Winfrey. Nothing prepared me for that moment, Gideon. You must remember, I don't watch TV and I missed your stint on her show, and it took me a moment to process what she was saying, when she said, Hello, I'm Oprah Winfrey. Hello, I said back to her in utter surprise and bewilderment, I'm Regina Blast. And then she must have asked me, Do you know someone by the name of Gideon Anderson? Of course, Gideon, I hadn't seen you in so many years that the mention of your name didn't ring a bell, so I told her, No, I don't think so, and I shook my head dubiously. Well he certainly knows you, Oprah said, laughing in the most gentle and loving fashion I have ever heard anyone laugh.

Yes, I told her, Regina, Oprah has a magnificence about her when you are with her in person that is hard to describe, and in my life I don't think I have ever encountered anyone who was so magnificent as her.

I agree, Gideon, Regina told me, she was absolutely magnificent and here she was standing with me in my studio, and I was surprised to see with my own eyes that I was taller than she, or rather that she was smaller than I am, for I am not that large, and though I didn't know how big Oprah might be in person, the fact that I was bigger than she, or rather that she was smaller than I was a true surprise and this surprise combined with her amazingly warm laugh made me like her instantly and that's when she told me about this man named Gideon Anderson who wrote a book *Gideon's Confession*, have I read it? Oprah asked. If I hadn't then I must know, she told me, that the book, *Gideon's Confession*, was one of the most beautiful and remarkable books that she, Oprah Winfrey, had ever read, and even though I had Gideon Anderson on my show, she told me, Regina told me that morning in the coffee shop, I don't know if the show itself, Oprah told Regina, if the exposure that my show might have brought to his book will be enough to sell copies of his book, because it is such a peculiar book celebrating, as I see it, Regina told me Oprah told her, a denial of the American success story, a rebuke, Oprah told Regina, of the so-called Horatio Alger story. And though the rebuke of *Gideon's Confession*, as Gideon Anderson writes his story, might manifest itself as the story of a young man who would prefer to sit all day long in the bar with an old-man mentor pouring him drinks, yet metaphorically speaking the rebuke of Gideon in his book, *Gideon's Confession*: his willingness to say no to all the trappings of the American dream; his rejection, for instance, of his girlfriend Claire's offer to bring him into her father's successful business, all of these things speak to me, Oprah Winfrey, because I as Oprah Winfrey, my brand of success, my race and gender, stand against everything Gideon rejects, and yet his rejection of all the things I stand for speaks to the deepest person of who I am: that person who, barely alive, exists fastened like a shrunken yet vestigial twin to this other person, Oprah Winfrey, who has achieved unbelievable levels of fame and fortune. And so she prattled on, Regina told me, still smitten by the time she spent with you, Gideon, having had lunch with her backstage. And she told me that the conversation the two of you shared was so intimate and touching that she didn't want it to end, but she also said that during the conversation and more to the point, during the filming of the show, you, Gideon, had mentioned me, Regina, and my artwork, and it was in this moment of your mention of me and my artwork when Oprah Winfrey determined that she wanted to visit my studio both to meet me and to see my artwork, and after this introduction where the two of us stood before each other, strangers to each other, even then I could tell that Oprah and I would soon become very intimate friends, but I showed her around my gallery and I attempted to describe for her what I was doing. At the time, I had moved to large-scale nine-foot-by-nine-foot square canvases and I had already developed my model of the white/black diptych painting that attempted to show both a certain illumination of light with the white canvas and the retinal response of that whiteness on the backside of the eyelid after the eyes had been closed, and while Oprah wandered around the space of my studio surveying various works of mine in different states of completion, I heard a small gasp come from her and a moment later Oprah was openly weeping in my studio so that I was stunned. I didn't know how I had gotten myself into this position. One moment I was alone in my studio working intensely on a painting, and the next moment, Oprah Winfrey was in my studio introducing herself to me, and mentioning you, Gideon, who, though you say you had spent all of your effort trying to forget me, I didn't have to spend much effort at all forgetting you, because at the time Oprah Winfrey made her introduction and told me how she came to know my art, the name Gideon Anderson rang a bell, but I couldn't place the name with a face, and when she mentioned that you had written a book, I still couldn't remember who you were by name, but when she told me that the memoir was written by a former University of Chicago student who once had an affair with me while also dating my best friend, then I remembered immediately who you were. And from this introduction, Oprah stood in the open space of my studio, and you haven't been to my studio, Gideon, and in fact very few people have ever stepped inside my studio and this is not because I view my studio as some sort of sacred and inviolate space, a temple to my painting, this thing I do with brush in hand smearing the canvas with paint, and at the time my smearing was either in white or it was in black and in either case I was trying to achieve the same effect: I was trying to figure out how to cancel out blackness with my white painting and I was also trying to figure out how to cancel whiteness with my black painting. I painted one painting to nullify the other painting which I painted to nullify the first painting. I was in a mood that though I use the word "nullification," because that is in fact the motive that was behind my painting, this demonic urge to nullify whiteness with blackness and blackness with whiteness, but my efforts felt less like nullification and more like immolation. It was as if I were trying through the power of my opposing images that were linked together, because they were by nature conjoined twins, but it was as if I were trying to strike some sort of spark by the combustible energy brought on by the frisson of these antinomies, this twinning, an energy that would somehow just cancel black and white out and reduce these noncolors but powerful social signifiers to a pile of meaningless ash and this process, at least as I construed it, could only happen through some sort of immolative process and while I wasn't interested in pyrotechnics and while I was interested in the alchemical power of art, I thought my idea rigorously applied might yield results, and so it was in the cauldron of these thoughts and ideas and experiments carried out in the confines of my studio where I committed myself to work, and I found that the work sustained me even though it was mostly solitary work, and by the nature of the work, I preferred occupying the space of my studio as a solitary person, and as a result, I have had very few guests enter into my studio space, and it was that day when Oprah Winfrey shocked me, inviting herself into my studio, and I was so unaccustomed to having guests in my studio space, but to have Oprah Winfrey herself somehow find and discover me in the space of my studio, and that she was occupying and sharing that space with me, and as we turned away from introductions and as she moved freely among my paintings I heard the asthmatic gasp, and then the weeping, and after a moment, she wiped her eyes, and she smiled at me rather radiantly, and she said, looking directly at me in the most uncannily intimate way that I have ever been looked at and she said to me, she, Oprah Winfrey, said, Regina, I think I get what you are trying to do here. I think I understand your artwork, and the reason why I think I understand your artwork, these black and white paintings and the way they try and cancel each other out, is because these paintings somehow understand me. It's as if your paintings are communicating directly with me and I in turn am communicating with them, and in my life, Regina, I don't think I have ever had an experience quite so powerful as the uncanny experience that I feel in the presence of your artwork, it's as if these paintings were designed to fit perfectly into the key hole of my innermost soul, and not only does the key fit, but it also turns and unlocks some inner lock that releases a sense in me that I somehow feel in all of the complex ways that I am a human being, that I am *understood*. So I hope you will accept my apologies for having an emotional outburst a moment ago, but you get me. And then she asked me if she might try and describe what she thought I was trying to do with my artwork, are you trying, Oprah Winfrey asked me, Regina told me that morning at the coffee shop, to juxtapose the opposing energies that somehow you are able to generate with your white and black paintings, energies of luminescence and absorption, and by juxtaposing those energies cause their cancellation, because I feel a power here, a sort of emotional heat coming off these black and white paintings and I can't quite locate where that emotional energy is coming from but I sense that it is coming from the remarkable and beautiful brushwork, but I sense that this energy is about a cancellation, a purification by fire, and a reduction of these two ideas to a pile of meaningless ash. Am I right, in your view, Regina, of my view of your art? And can you believe it, Gideon, Regina told me, that one minute I was alone in my studio and the next moment Oprah Winfrey was in my studio explaining to me the exact terms of my artwork back to me. It felt like an uncanny miracle and I didn't know what I had done to deserve it, but I suppose I owe at least a little bit of thanks to you and to that memoir of yours and to the fact that not only did you accurately describe my paintings in your book, but you were also kind enough to mention me to Oprah Winfrey, and by so doing, you effectively changed my life, because in a moment of time I went from a person painting light and sunsets to a person dedicated to trying to create my own energy through these black and white paintings, and then I had Oprah in my studio and while she was in my studio, and not knowing how to respond to her or how to express my gratitude for her miraculous arrival in my studio, I asked her if she would mind sitting on a stool in the center of my studio so that I could draw a sketch of her, and believe it or not, Gideon, Oprah obliged me. She sat down on the stool and positioned herself until she was comfortable. I sat on a stool opposite her and with a sheet of paper that I had cut to a nine-inch-by-nine-inch shape, I began to sketch her. When I make art, Gideon, I am silent, because I am directing all of my energy to receiving impulses through all of my senses and particularly through my eyes, and I try to record the impact of these sensory inputs on my psychology. My pencil records the impressions the external world makes on my sensibility with the same sensitivity that an EKG records the minute vibrations of the heart or if you want to speak on geologic scale with the sensitivity that a seismometer records the distant rumblings and vibrations of Earth's mantle. Oprah sat on a stool in my studio and she stared at me as if she herself were a subject in a Vermeer painting, her face cast slightly over her shoulder, and her eyes looking directly at me caused some slight perturbation in me and I attempted to register that in my sketch of her. While I was drawing her, in the light of my studio, and until you see my studio, Gideon, you have no idea how lucky I am to have such a studio. My studio is located right on the south branch of the Chicago River near the St. Charles Air Line Bridge at 1500 S. Lumber Street, and as such, it picks up an eerie radiance of light reflected by the waves of the river onto the ceiling and walls of my studio, and that day, in the brightness of my studio, a very prim yet beautiful Oprah Winfrey stared at me over her shoulder and if I said she was challenging me by the way she looked at me, I would be misstating it. What she seemed to be doing in her look at me was encouraging me to get beyond the commodified persona of Oprah Winfrey and all of the millions of images of her that have flooded the zone and to find through my eye and my hand some essential quality, some private as yet undisclosed secret about her that none of the cameras and magazine covers and TV shows and the endless recorded filmography have revealed; that vast proliferation and projection of the product Oprah Winfrey into the land of, shall we call it, Empire Oprah, which our world perforce has become, and she, Oprah Winfrey, the living person sitting on the stool in my studio, was the endless reproducing source of that great wealth and power of imagery and she was exhorting me that afternoon to go find an unturned stone. Please, she seemed to say to me, if you, Regina Blast, can find one unturned stone in this vast echo chamber of my endlessly repeating self, please overturn it, and show me what lies beneath. And while I sat there sketching Oprah, I sensed a gap in the armature of Oprah swinging slightly open and from the small triangular gap of that door's opening I was able to catch a glimpse of the bottomless depths of her loving humanity and I can tell you this right now, Gideon, in all of my life, I have never come close to encountering a person who, like Oprah, possessed such a bottomless depth of humanity and understanding and lovingness and I say this now, of course, because I've had many years to reflect on that afternoon and I've had the opportunity to compare the events of that afternoon to all the other events of all the other afternoons that I have lived through and all of the people that I have encountered, and thinking of it now from this perspective I can tell you that I only feel a deeper awe of Oprah Winfrey now than I did that afternoon she visited me on a whim in my studio. I felt awed by the total human radiance that she seemed to emit when she opened for my eyes only ever so slightly that door, and through the small triangular gap of that door, I seemed to witness eternity.

When we were done, Oprah stood up from her stool, and she stretched, and she came over to see what I had drawn, and she smiled at me and placed her hand on my shoulder and she said, Is this what you saw? Is this it?

Yes, I told her. This is it. This is what I saw.

But, Oprah said, slightly alarmed, the amount of gestures that you seemed to make while you were drawing me, it seemed like you were recording more than just this simple, yet I dare say, perfect shape. You looked, Regina, like you had been performing tai chi or something and I had expected more.

At this, Oprah Winfrey laughed and I laughed. And then she said, so be it, Regina. I will carry this drawing with me as the one undisclosed secret that is left of the private person that I once was before the cameras started capturing me on film. Then looking at the picture I had drawn of her a bit more carefully, she let out a small gasp, and then she told me that she was wrong to judge my work so quickly. She told me that upon second look my drawing of her was one of the most powerful images that anyone has ever made of her and it was made more powerful by the fact that my witnessing of her was not only brutally honest and direct, but that I wasn't looking at her through a lens but with my own eye studying her over the course of an hour.

I thanked Oprah for understanding and then I signed the drawing for her and I gave it to her as a gift and at that moment she hugged and thanked me. She told me that my secret was safe with her and that the drawing I had made of her would be privately displayed in the most intimate room of her house so that it would be a drawing for her eyes only and for those of her most intimate companions. Then she told me she must be going but that she would be back soon. For what reason, I had no idea. But I watched her leave my studio and into the black SUV she went and in a moment she was gone and I was left bewildered sitting on that stool in my studio wondering what had just happened to me.

S hall we call it, I asked Regina, the Perturbation of Oprah Winfrey? She is an irresistible force unto herself, and one falls into her orbit by accident or will to be changed forever by the encounter. In my case it was as much accident I suppose as it was in your case, but in both cases, our falling into Oprah's orbit would not have happened had I not written my book, and having written my book, I should have listened to my instincts and tossed it in Lake Michigan where it belonged rather than to the cajoling of that Kentucky gentleman and lawyer who prosecuted Khmer Rouge war criminals at The Hague, and whom I had met because I had been seated next to him at a dinner party and having had too much bourbon I spouted off about my manuscript, which I described as a turd, which he thought was the funniest thing that he had ever heard in his life, and he too was as drunk as I was for we were drinking Kentucky bourbon in tumblers with ice one after the other and we both stared luridly eye to eye as we sank into drunkenness and exchanged the inanities that pass for conversation while drunk, and it was in this state of drunkenness that he suggested to his agent that he read my manuscript, and the next day, still hungover and still quite possibly drunk, in a moment of weakness, I sent my manuscript off to the agent, rather than waiting for the storm-seized waters of Lake Michigan to foment into a froth so that I might send this, *The Ark of Disquiet*, my private manuscript listing all the things of my life I had wanted to purge myself of from that final year at the University of Chicago, and once I dropped the manuscript into the mailbox and off to the agent, rather than the nothing that I assumed would become of this act, a rising crescendo of everything imaginable and not so imaginable began to happen to me, all of which is so regrettable that even now I feel a deep compulsion to write another book filling it with all the bile that the first book and all of the publicity and *The Oprah Winfrey Show* and the musical has subsequently filled me with and rather than publishing it, I would instead follow through on my original intention to toss it into the waves of Lake Michigan and purge myself once and for all of all the bile.

You could call that manuscript *The Return of the Slacker King*, Regina said, and Regina smiled at me when she said this in quite a charming way and I was reminded again of our tryst together seventeen years ago, and even slightly further back than that, I remembered the moment in the restaurant where I had been sitting with my then girlfriend, Claire, and in walked her best friend, Regina, who, as I later wrote of her in my original *The Ark of Disquiet* which became *Gideon's Confession*, "wore jackboots, had butch hair, and sported a sleeveless T-shirt with army surplus cargo pants," but little did I know that I was describing a young woman who was at the advent of her own nascent journey to becoming an artist and I felt it that very moment in the coffee shop with Regina that morning, a retrospective disgust at myself for having written those words as a descriptor of the woman, Regina Blast, and an even greater retrospective disgust at having also published those words making them the durable public statement that they have become in the wake of my own book's durable popularity.

The thing is, I told Regina, there were several things that happened as a result of my appearance on *The Oprah Winfrey Show* just after the publication of my novel, *Gideon's Confession*. The first thing that happened, and it was something that I should have predicted, but somehow I had failed to predict it, was that my appearance on *The Oprah Winfrey Show* made me and my book, *Gideon's Confession*, instantly famous. Here's where we get to the concept, shall we call it, the Perturbation of Oprah Winfrey—or perhaps even closer to the point, the perturbation of O? Because here's the thing, Regina, Oprah gave me two things that I wouldn't exchange for anything in the world; the first was our conversation over shrimp scampi before the filming of her show, and the second thing she gave me was that brief dance upon the live stage of her televised show. I wouldn't swap either of these experiences for anything in the world because they fundamentally changed me as a person. These two moments in Oprah Winfrey's presence are absolutely singular experiences in my life, and what I gained from them was a sense of how deep a connection, far deeper than I ever thought possible, one person can make with another. Here we were, Oprah Winfrey and Gideon Anderson, absolute strangers to each other, in fact, we were antipodes of each other, and yet over the course of an hour, she built a connecting bridge of such emotional power and depth between us that it changed who I was as a person. If I now sit in silent meditation as you just moments ago encountered me, Regina, trying to retain the vision of this beautiful garden outside the window of the coffee shop on the inside of my eyelids, thereby attempting to extract as much joy as such a garden might impart to my sensory system, then that is because Oprah taught me that I had a sensory system that was capable of sounding the deep chasms of joy that lie submerged in my own human heart. Oprah taught me that I was capable of experiencing simple human joy. In exchange for this experience, she also imparted the nightmare of fame upon me, but this was not her fault. Of course, it may have been the result of her charisma that like the sun that you were just describing to me, that balances on the horizon thereby flooding the zone with light, so too did Oprah Winfrey's charisma necessarily flood the zone and she flooded it with an incandescent charismatic power that was not very different from the sun's illumination, and its power, her power to attract, is as irresistible as that flower's power to attract the bumblebee buzzing around its pistil and stamen collecting golden pollen on its forelegs and hindlegs. That being said, I got caught in the glare of Oprah Winfrey's charisma, and because I was proximally close to her radiance, and since my proximity to Oprah was captured on camera for all the world to see while we danced our two-step waltz, I picked up a bit of the remnant power of her charisma and the fame machine suddenly lit up around me. I became the object of its gaze. Now, Regina, I must tell you that I am one

of those rare American individuals who has never wanted
fame or fortune; in fact, my book, *Gideon's Confession*, is essentially my personal polemic against all things having to do
with traditional notions of success, and it is also, you might
say, a slightly exaggerated celebration of slothfulness, of doing
nothing for the sake of doing nothing: it is the epitaph of a
flaneur; it is an ode and a paean to failure, it is a vital portrait
of a loser who is happy with being a loser, and it tries to capture the inner spirit and thinking of a young man who prefers
to say "fuck you" to the American ethos of success and it is
also the portrait of a person who prefers rather to drift with
utter nonchalance down the bumpy and at times fraught current of life no matter that there is a perilous waterfall just
around the next bend in the river; so, having written such a
book about a young person who was content to live a useless
life of anonymity it came as a surprise to me, after appearing
on *The Oprah Winfrey Show* that afternoon, how swiftly fame
and fortune found me. My book became an instant best-
seller, and since its days on the best-seller list it has had a long
successful run. I've become slightly rich from the royalties,
and there have been several editions of the book, the most re-
cent one of which has been printed with a laudable introduction by that Kentucky gentleman who himself went on to pen
a trilogy of famous memoirs (1) of his boyhood in Kentucky,
(2) of his Ivy League student years, and (3) of his subsequent
brilliant trial career as a prominent lawyer bringing Khmer
Rouge war criminals to justice at The Hague, but he in his
introduction to the latest edition of my book describes in his
own peculiarly charming and humorous way how the publication of *Gideon's Confession* had come about: he described

the dinner where we were seated at a crowded table cheek and jowl, he described the jokes back and forth, the generational difference between us but the connection that I had made with him, and he noted that very few people in his orbit had ever made such a connection with him as the connection that I made with him because in general and for reasons the Kentucky gentleman couldn't quite explain, people naturally felt intimidated in his presence. It was something he was always consciously trying to reduce, people's natural sense of fear while in his presence. But what was so remarkable about me, the Kentucky gentleman went on to write in the introduction to the latest edition of my book, *Gideon's Confession*, was that I showed no sign of fear or intimidation when I first encountered him and as a result an easy rapport just naturally sprang up between us, and the Kentucky gentleman went on to write how moved he was by my ability to engage with him on a person-to-person basis, and then he described the bourbon, and the lurid eye-to-eye laughter, and the sudden revelation that sitting next to him was a writer, because I had told him in my drunkenness that I had penned a stupid memoir that I had written for the sole purpose of hurling it, the manuscript, like a turd upon the storm-tossed waters of Lake Michigan, and rather than losing a potentially great work of literature to an impetuous hurling of the book turd into the waters of Lake Michigan, the Kentucky gentleman told me that I should instead send the book to his agent, which I did, and from there all the rest of the story of my life unfolds, the second part of my life, that is, which is still unfolding; the first part of my life, that wonderful life I had when I was an unknown and unwanted person living a life of blissful anonymity, has vanished forever from my grasp—that was the gist of the introduction to the latest edition of *Gideon's Confession*, and maybe what lies beneath all of my problems is a personality characteristic that the Kentucky gentleman identifies in me: an ability to establish an easy rapport with people that has brought me more friends than I ever wanted.

All of this fame was brought to my book by Oprah Winfrey, and more particularly it came to me as a result of that small, brief waltz I had with Oprah, and her dubbing of me as the Slacker King or King of Slack, but it all changed my life forever, because here's the thing, Regina, that dance was such a spontaneous dance, so spur of the moment, and though much of what appears on Oprah seems spur of the moment, I've also been told that the structure of the show, the rhythm and cadence of the show and the way the show moves between its live audience and its commercial breaks is actually tightly choreographed, but the one dance that she did with me, that moment of the dance was no more choreographed than the dance itself, and as soon as it started it was over and we went back to the business at hand which was the conversation about my book filmed in front of that live studio audience. However, because the dance was such an exceptional and unexpected moment on Oprah Winfrey's show, and because just after that dance Oprah referred to me as the Slacker King and then as the King of Slack and then again, and there is tape evidence to support this, as "my" King of Slack and coming as all this came after her mentioning that we had shared some intimate moments backstage before the show, but there was just enough innuendo in the triangulation of these facts to start the whole rumor mill gossiping and before I knew it first one paparazzo—a strange guy in a black fedora who jumped out the side door of a car and snapped several pictures of me with a camera that had a huge lens while I was walking down Sangamon Street, but then later there were several more paparazzi, all of them jumping out at me to snap pictures of me and then there were others who snapped pictures of me from telescoping lenses where they, the paparazzi or paparazzo, depending on whether they were working in group formation as was often the case or rather as lone wolves, were hiding in safe locations and so I was unaware of the fact that pictures were being snapped of me and when I was aware of the paparazzi I still didn't know why these strange people were taking pictures of me, and before I knew it these clandestine photos and images of me started to show up on the front pages of all the gossip magazines, and the *National Enquirer* was the chief proponent of the theory that I, Gideon Anderson, was somehow Oprah Winfrey's clandestine love object, and the headlines, the crazy headlines, there was for instance, in the *National Enquirer*, I'll never forget, the headline "The Slacker King Slays the Queen of Talk" and underneath was a blurry doctored photograph showing the two of us, Oprah Winfrey and me, joined in an illicit romantic embrace. Another, *People* magazine's infamously headlined "The King of Slack, Gideon, Woos Oprah with Waltz: The Story behind the Story." Only there was no story, all the stories as they pertained to Oprah and me were fabrications, and I somehow or another got caught up in the whirlwind of the zeitgeist. I was for a brief moment, the "zeit" and the "geist." All of this was incredibly devastating to me because I somehow felt culpable for the unwanted attention, and I felt that the unwanted attention had fueled what I could only imagine was a horrifying controversy from Oprah Winfrey's perspective. It was as if she had suffered not one but several lapses of professional judgment. In my view, the first lapse of judgment that Oprah Winfrey exhibited as pertains to me was when she read a book, *Gideon's Confession*, by an unknown, unvetted author, me, Gideon Anderson, a book I should add, that was published by an unknown unvetted publisher, Noname Press—because frankly, all of the books that Oprah Winfrey typically reads and promotes on her show are books published by known publishing houses, and since these publishing houses carefully and for the most part though not always vet their authors, she can have some reasonable confidence when bringing these vetted authors onto her stage to promote their work that they will act according to the standard protocol of a book author tour that converges with the publicity machine of *The Oprah Winfrey Show*. But in my case Oprah made the mistake of bringing an unknown and unvetted author, me, Gideon Anderson, onto her show, and the reason she did this, she later told me backstage while we were having lunch, shrimp scampi, was because my book had touched her and she wanted to meet me and talk to me about it in private and the only way she could talk to me privately was to invite me onto her show and so an invitation was extended to me via my publicist and with that invitation came an additional invitation to join her for lunch at Harpo Studios on Sangamon Street on the Near West Side an hour before the show started, and her extension of this lunch invitation to me was, in my view, another one of her professional misjudgments because as you, Regina, just said to me about letting a fox be a fox but in somebody else's henhouse, well, Oprah had invited me, an unvetted author and an unknown person, a feral animal so to speak, or in fact the fox that you claim that I am, but she invited me into her own so-called backstage henhouse and it was here in this so-called henhouse where she, Oprah Winfrey, and I, Gideon Anderson, connected directly as two people might connect over a lunch, only the asymmetry between who she, Oprah Winfrey, is, and who I, Gideon Anderson, am, and the vast gulf that naturally separates the famous person from the unknown person, this vast unbridgeable distance was somehow collapsed the moment we met. It was my easy rapport with her, a personality characteristic later identified by that Kentucky gentleman in his introduction to my book, but it was my ease in the presence of others that allowed me quite simply to extend my hand to Oprah and say hello and I sensed in that moment a bit of confusion, let's call it the initial perturbation both from Oprah and from myself that we, she Oprah and me Gideon, had so instantly become so unguarded with each other. It was a shock to both of us and a wonder. In fact, during that lunch Oprah had confessed to me how strange it had felt to her to feel so suddenly on an equal and intimate footing with a stranger, and she said that what she noticed about me from the very start was that I possessed a certain guilelessness upon confronting her fame. It was as if I didn't recognize who she, Oprah Winfrey, was or what she represented; as if I had only seen her as a stranger and her recognition that I didn't appear to recognize her but that I had seen her only as a stranger gave her a moment to see herself through the eyes of someone who didn't immediately recognize her as the mega-star Oprah Winfrey that she was, and it had been years, she told me, since she hadn't been immediately recognized as the star Oprah Winfrey by someone and that experience alone, that it should have happened at all, perturbed and excited her. It was as if I had seen her, Oprah Winfrey, with a kind of polarized eyeglass lens that had filtered out all of the fame that she naturally emits; and by this filtering process I was able to see her not as the monstrously famous, deeply charismatic human being that she, Oprah Winfrey, in fact is, but rather that I, Gideon Anderson, was able to witness her simply as the human being that she had once been prior to the onslaught of her life after she had become Oprah Winfrey. It was as if I were seeing the Oprah Winfrey person before she ever became Oprah Winfrey, and this encounter of hers, with a person like me, who saw her as a person, well she didn't have these sorts of encounters anymore. She was struck, upon meeting me, by how she felt as if she were meeting an old long-lost friend from her past, and that old friend she told me whom she was meeting for the first time in a very long time was none other than her old pre-famous self. It's the funniest thing, Gideon, Oprah told me over shrimp scampi in her so-called henhouse, I feel like my old self talking to you and I can't tell you how good that makes me feel. I so very much miss my old self, shall we call her, that old self, oprah with a small *o* but do you know, Gideon, that that old self is so far gone that no matter how much I wish to call her, small-*o* oprah, back from the past she will never arrive, but it's in rare moments with guileless people such as yourself who seem somehow immune from the soul-shaking, terrible excitement that seems to grip everyone who ever meets me but it's from guileless people like you who see me as a stranger, when

I get a brief glimpse of small-*o* oprah dancing alone by herself in that dark wood.

This luncheon meeting with Oprah, I told Regina, made Oprah so joyful, I could see it in her body language and I could see it in the way that she engaged with me, so when we went onstage in front of that live audience her joy just overflowed and in the spontaneity of her warm emotion toward me she asked me to dance with her a two-step waltz and while we danced the two-step in front of the live audience and the dance, you know, it was broadcast literally to tens of millions of people, and in that public arena there was an intimacy that we, Oprah Winfrey and me, Gideon Anderson, shared, the small private gap of space opening between our two bodies and closing between us as we swayed gently to the music, but in the private space of our own intimacy I knew I was dancing not with the mega-star Oprah Winfrey, but with a person who had long ago vanished from the world, small-*o* oprah, and she too knew that it was small-*o* oprah who had appeared on stage to dance a two-step with me, Gideon Anderson, of all people! And then she was gone, small-*o* oprah vanished, and Oprah Winfrey reappeared on stage and the moment of intimacy passed and that's when we took our seats opposite each other to begin our conversation about *Gideon's Confession* in earnest.

But it was this request of Oprah Winfrey's that I dance with her that was her third professional misjudgment; and it was the combination of these three professional misjudgments as well as her underestimation of how her language use particularly with the possessive "my," as in "my Slacker King," and her behavior during the two-step waltz, but it was

Oprah Winfrey's underestimation of how these small little irregular and spontaneous things broadcast to tens of millions of people would play out for me. Maybe it was her disregard for the strict formal protocols of her show, and her desire to see small-*o* oprah appear on her show for just a moment that overwhelmed the executive function of her thinking, but these small acts caused fame to happen to me, and who am I other than quite literally an innocent bystander who happened to write an idiotic book that I should have never published, but having published it I was drawn almost inexorably into Oprah's orbit, as if the immensity of her fame had a planetary mass equal to Jupiter and as if I were some small particle of space debris that was brought crashingly down from some unknown zenith or rather from the zenith of anonymity plunging into the white-hot nadir of her fame bubble; and just moments after that small two-step waltz occurred and when the final curtain dropped on my segment of *The Oprah Winfrey Show*, I was transformed from the nobody that I had always wanted to be into an avatar of fame but an avatar whose fame was parasitical upon Oprah Winfrey's fame. It was a fame that didn't issue sui generis from me but rather it was a narrative construct of the fame machine that collected against my will, around me; the fame machine snapping pictures of me and publishing insane and improbable narratives of someone who looked like me, my fame avatar, but who wasn't me, but who had a life of his own and who may have had or who might be having an intimate relationship with Oprah Winfrey. My fame avatar, in other words, was developing a life of its own with improbably ridiculous stories associated with it, and as this fame avatar was essentially my simulacrum or doppelgänger, which is what it often felt like to me that it was, I was caught up in the drama of its story. What's more, because my fame avatar wasn't a construct of my own doing, but because it was an inadvertent construct of Oprah Winfrey's doing, and maybe because I was somehow complicit or collaborative in my fame avatar's construction since I had guilelessly danced that two-step waltz with small-*o* oprah, I naturally came to worry that my fame avatar somehow implicated Oprah Winfrey or rather shadowed her or rather I worried that my fame avatar cast a negative shadow upon her fame in the form of the small so-called love scandal that was now blowing up on all of the gossip rags on the magazine racks.

Quite frankly, Regina, I can't tell you how horrified I was by all of this. I felt I had been strategically stupid. I had been naïve, an oaf, an idiot who didn't know what he was getting into. I was deeply concerned that my guileless participation on *The Oprah Winfrey Show* precipitated the birth of my fame avatar and simultaneously ended my private unknown life forever.

I had been unprepared for my meeting with Oprah, and I had been unprepared for the show. There is sartorial evidence to support my case. My khaki cotton slacks, for instance, hadn't been properly tailored and the cuffs of my pants fell beneath my shoe heels, which caused the cuff fabric to fray. My shoes, loafers, were preposterously worn out and unpolished and I was wearing an ill-fitting cheap blue blazer that I had purchased at a discount from Men's Warhorse specifically for what I thought was going to be a small publicity tour that I was told would attend the publication of my book, my original, *The Ark of Disquiet*, which my publisher had forced me to rename against my will, *Gideon's Confession*, but I certainly didn't and wasn't prepared for something as radically unexpected as an invitation to appear on *The Oprah Winfrey Show*, so, because I was unprepared for all of this, my approach going into the event was to be as nonchalant as possible. I was the author, after all, of a frivolous book, and if that book had one lesson to tell the world it was that the only true way to find happiness or at least a sort of situational easefulness in the world was by not caring about the big stuff or the small stuff, but now, retrospectively, after appearing on *The Oprah Winfrey Show* and after becoming the object of a rapidly metastasizing gossip machine that speculated endlessly upon what the true relationship might be between Oprah Winfrey and her Slacker King, I worried that my guileless and shambolic comportment that day had been the wrong strategy. It was as if I had entered the inner garden, unveiled in priestly raiment, and thus having entered, I had been struck by a power greater than my comprehension and that power blasted me or rather it blasted some rumored avatar of me kaleidoscopically out into manifold and sundry dimensions. At that moment I felt I had left home for good, ousted, never to return.

Thankfully, for me, Gideon, Regina said, my encounter with Oprah didn't initially blast me out of the stratosphere, as your encounter seems to have done to you. In my case, Oprah had shown up at my studio out of the blue. I was so startled when she rang my bell that my paintbrush jumped off track and marred the painting that I had been working on. Then Oprah Winfrey, of all people, walked into my studio and she told me things of my paintings that were just as true as the things that you, Gideon, had written of my paintings in your book. It was as if Oprah not only understood the paintings that were in my studio and which I had made, but it was as if she understood who I was as a painter, and as I told you if you were to ask me who I am, I would tell you that I am a painter who attempts to paint one way or the other the light either as it filters into my studio or as it registers on my sensory system leaving a fading retinal impression that glimmers like a sun of my own making on the backside of my eyelids. But if you ask me who I am not, I would tell you as I have told you already, that I am not a person who is not a painter, so when Oprah Winfrey came into my studio and stood looking at my paintings, and while I stood watching her look at my paintings, and then when I heard her emotional gasp, an almost barely contained sorrowful expression that mixed the fleeting joy of life with the bitter sadness of the tragic fallenness of the world, this idea that we live briefly and die forever, I heard all this in her sob that afternoon, Gideon, and then there was that moment when Oprah turned and looked upon me with the naked radiance of her gaze, and in that moment, in the radiance of her gaze, she, Oprah Winfrey, seemed to apprehend me in my wholeness and completeness both as an artist and as a person. In other words, it felt as if she not only understood the canvases, my black and white nine-by-nine diptychs, but as if she understood me, the artist and human being who had been painting from an inner compulsion these paintings.

I had followed my painterly obsessions as fanatically as I dared ever since I was an undergraduate at the University of Chicago, and in a way, Gideon, this application of paint to the canvas wherein I attempt to find the bliss of my own eternity by means of my own brushstrokes as they touch the canvas, though I do it with my eyes open, yet my pursuit of this obsession is also blind and monomaniacal. I don't know why I do what I do, nor do I know what it means that I do what I do, nor do I know what it says about me as a person that I do this thing I do painting obsessively at these canvases, nor do I understand who I am as I relate to the world outside the confines of my studio because really, Gideon, when I am outside my studio and when I am not engaged with my artwork, then I truly feel as if I am a nonperson who is adrift and without identity in the world. I carry this overwhelming sense with me when I am outside my studio that I am a negative, a zero, a void, an absence, or in a word I feel worthless and a nothing, and these feelings, Gideon, if you want to know the truth, are the very things that those runic symbols that I have tattooed on my body and that you carelessly wrote about in your book, but it is these feelings that these mysterious tattooed symbols try to give voice to.

These all are aspects of myself that I don't understand or comprehend and thus, the runic symbols are a textual form of what I find inscrutable in me; they are symbols that are themselves unsayable and as such they perfectly express why I feel the way I do when I am not directly engaged with the making of my art. These runic symbols draw upon me as a vacuum that threatens to suck me completely from the face of the Earth. I feel this vacuum. I hear its hum, yet I don't understand it nor do I know why I hear it only when I am not engaged with my painting.

However, Oprah looked upon me with a sort of naked radiance in her aspect that seemed to take me completely in: both the me that is the painter who paints these canvases, and the me who is not a painter and who is therefore nothing, and the other me that is ignorant to both the causes that motivate the painter to paint what the painter paints and the person who when the painter is not painting feels a nothing that only runic symbols can represent. In other words, Gideon, it was the first time in my life when someone, in this case Oprah Winfrey, apprehended the totality of who I am as a person in the world. It was as if she had read the runes that were tattooed on my skin and she understood their literal meaning... even if I didn't understand their meaning... and in that moment of comprehension it was the first time in my whole life, Gideon, I had felt loved.

Did you actually expose yourself to Oprah so that she saw your tattoos, Regina? Because if I remember, those so-called runic symbols were tattooed from your back around your midriff and onto your belly.

No, I didn't show Oprah my actual tattoos, Gideon, Regina told me. I didn't need to show Oprah my tattoos because for one you had written about my tattoos in your book which Oprah had read carefully enough so as to be able to track me down and find me in my new studio, and for two having read your book so carefully, naturally Oprah would have known that the runic symbols were a tattooed feature of my skin, as everyone else who has read your book or seen the musical or who has watched the cult movie *The Slacker King* would be well aware of. Can you believe, Gideon, that you wrote about my tattoos in the pages of your book, which may have taken you all of a minute to write, and then what you went on to publish was not only a confession of your own privacies but also a confession of my privacies, and I don't know what gave you the right, other than the fact that you actually saw my tattoos when we shared a private moment, but to make manifest for the whole world and for the duration of my life and beyond what was meant literally only for me, my own private tattoos whose meaning was as inscrutable to me as my own meaning to myself was is something that you should never be forgiven for.

But that being said, Oprah's apprehension of me on the other hand was so objective and complete that she accepted and understood me in my wholeness; this apprehension of hers for me felt in addition to everything else as if she were reading directly the runic codes tattooed on my skin which were hidden from her view; but I could tell that she understood that I was someone who would have such tattoos tattooed on my skin and she would understand why I needed to have such tattoos tattooed on my skin and she would know the pain that I felt that my private tattoos had been made public for all of the world to see in their own imagination because of that book you wrote and published. She, Oprah, understood everything including what the precise meaning of my runic code was saying. So yes, rather than your experience where you felt transfigured into an avatar that was then jettisoned from what you call your home and blasted through the gossip magazines into the stratosphere rebranded not as Gideon Anderson who has an agency of your own, but as the Slacker King whose value in the world is dependent on five minutes that you shared with Oprah Winfrey on a TV show wherein you did an impromptu dance, I felt, to the contrary, as if Oprah Winfrey had entered my studio by stealth and found this alien creature, me, who had not yet found a home in the world and who had therefore isolated herself in her studio pursuing a fanatical artistic vision, but Oprah Winfrey found me where I was and redirected me to my own home. She helped me understand what the meaning of the tattoos was and she also understood the pain that your revelation of my tattoos in the pages of your book caused for me. Perhaps that was the meaning of her gasp, because she understood not only my painting but she understood me and why I had had my tattoos tattooed on my body and why I had subsequently lived in a self-imposed solitary isolation in my studio once your book had been published and my secrets had been exposed for all the world to see.

And then Oprah was gone with the drawing that I had made of her with the promise to return. I looked out my studio window down at the street below where Oprah returned to the black SUV, the driver holding the door open for her, and just before she got in the car she glanced back up at the window and seeing me looking down at her, she waved and mouthed words which I could distinctly read—*thank you*— and then she got in the car, the door was shut, the driver got in the SUV, and off they went, disappearing around the corner. The light in my studio flickered as a veil of dark clouds passed overhead and it registered on my consciousness only as the changing tonality of light. Did this really happen? Why did it happen? How did it happen? My mind buzzed with a flurry of questions. Oprah Winfrey's visit had felt so improbable and dreamlike. It was not merely an afternoon interlude, but Oprah's visit felt like an interlude that occurred in the middle of the wilderness that was my solitary existence at that time. Oprah's visit, brief though it was, filled me with hopeful premonitions. Happiness started to fill my heart. I was visited by the great Oprah Winfrey and she understood who I was and the pain that I had suffered as a result of the publication of your book. The improbability of her visit, the dreamlike quality, the benevolence of her gaze upon me, her total and objective apprehension of who I was, and the opening of the floodgates that that apprehension had triggered, the sense flooding in upon me, that with that singular objective and appraising gaze, Oprah had understood all that I was and accepted all that I was, an acceptance of me that was both tender and kindly, but I felt awash in Oprah's benevolent and loving kindness and then her sudden disappearance with the promise that she would one day return, it all felt suddenly like a humorous joke, and I couldn't stop myself from laughing at the absurdity and at the joy of it. There I was all alone in my studio and for several minutes I just stood there in the window laughing overwhelmed with joy. When I was done laughing, I went back to work.

I cut a nine-by-nine sheet of drawing paper, and I attempted to remember the total sequence of hand gestures during my drawing session of Oprah. And then I tried to re-create as accurately as I could the exact gestural order of hand movements that produced the original drawing that I had made of Oprah. As I repeated each gesture I moved my hand directing the pencil across the paper. I remember Oprah's eyes exhorting me, See me as no one else has seen me, Regina, capture me as I am with your pencil. As I followed the sequence of hand gestures best that I could remember, I looked toward the stool where Oprah Winfrey had just been sitting moments ago staring over her shoulder at me looking very similar to a Black version, an Oprah version, of the model in Vermeer's painting *Girl with a Pearl Earring*. Oprah was wearing a large-cut blue sapphire earring on each ear and the sapphire glowed with a blue radiance that seemed to light up my studio, and Oprah's gaze was so direct and open it was as if she were exhorting me, a stranger, to come close to her, to come closer still, to inch ever so closely to the point of periapsis so that we—she, Oprah Winfrey, and I, Regina Blast—might, stripped of our names, close the gap that naturally separates strangers, but she encouraged me to walk the small span of space from me to her, and Please, she seemed to say to me, please, gaze into the tunnels of my eyes, Regina, and be lost in a windblown world of breaking hopes and a shipwrecked country of green blue dreams, and that afternoon while I drew her, while we sat across from each other as nameless strangers might sit across from each other, I took her invitation and I fell deep into the well of her eyes until I was indeed lost in a shipwrecked country of green blue dreams and the light in my studio was filled with a blue radiance as sunlight passed through the faceted sapphire gems dangling from her ears, and as I drew her, and then later as I repeated the gestural sequence of hand movements thereby re-creating the original drawing of Oprah, I swore that what I was drawing with my pencil alone was indeed the light, that blue radiance, the transcendent and sparkling blue, and when I was finished with my drawing, and in a fashion similar to William Blake whose work is also at the Tate but in an attempt to memorialize the words that had entered into my mind as I was drawing Oprah, I scrawled along the edges of the drawing the words *gaze into the tunnels of my eyes and be lost in a windblown world of breaking hopes and a shipwrecked country of green blue dreams*, and then I handed the drawing over to Oprah, and she gasped again as she apprehended what I had created and without saying so much as *I will be back*, and then *Thank you*, she was out my door, but after she left, and as I redrew her, re-creating with absolute accuracy the exact sequence of gestures that had caused me to create the blue drawing of Oprah, even though the drawing was made with the blackest charcoal pencil, I saw again Oprah sitting on my stool, and I could swear I saw it again, the blue radiance filling my studio, and I felt it again, her benevolent and loving kindness falling upon me, and when I finished my re-creation of the blue Oprah drawing drawn with the same black charcoal pencil, I noticed that it too seemed to glimmer, albeit subtly as if it, the charcoal drawing, were itself capable of transmitting the spectral color blue and I knew then that what Oprah meant when she said that she would be back was that she would never be back and that we would never meet again, yet so long as I re-created with gestural fidelity the exact sequence of hand movements that had led to the creation of that first Oprah drawing, she would return again and again, there on my empty stool in the center of my studio to gaze upon me in a radiant blue light of loving kindness inviting me to fall into her world as if into an endless embrace.

When I was done with the second drawing of Oprah which was exactly the same as the first drawing of Oprah, I scrawled more words upon the drawing. I scrawled the words upon the drawing not as an act of defilement, but as an act of remembrance and thought. I wrote: *the act of benevolent kindness begins with the open eyes of love*, and I then repeated yet again, in a new third drawing, the gestural sequence of movements that had led to the creation of the original drawing and of the second drawing, which I had copied from memory, remembering not merely the image that I had drawn of Oprah, but remembering the exact gestural hand sequence and repeating it, and as I drew her a third time, I felt it again, as if I, through a precise sequence of gestures with a charcoal pencil, were conjuring forth Oprah Winfrey in all of her manifest beauty and in the full objective range of all of her meanings not least of which seemed to be her ability to understand me in the full range of my objective meanings, and this coming together of her gaze upon me as my gaze fell upon her while I performed that precise sequence of hand gestures caused the floodgates of love to swing open in my studio and as I drew her a third time following that gestural sequence she looked at me from the stool in my studio and she exhorted me yet again to draw her, to find by drawing her, her own runic code that said beyond saying precisely who she was in her totality which included an all-comprehending sense of who I was in my totality; to see her and to re-create her as no one had ever seen her and certainly as no one had seen her who had only seen her through a camera's lens or through the camera's endlessly duplicatable imagery. I am the most known person in the world, Oprah seemed to say to me from the stool where she sat in the center of my studio; my com-modified image has re-created the world into Oprah Winfrey land, but I am also the most knowing person and it is my wish, Regina, Oprah seemed to say to me, that you, through your artistry show both the known and unknown totality of Oprah. That's when she turned her body slightly askance to the axis line which I saw rising from the ground where her feet were positioned to slightly above the top of her head, and which I saw not merely as an axis but as the possible diameter that formed an invisible circle that enclosed all of Oprah, and within that circle and with her head tilted askance to the axis line so that to see me she had to cast her glance at me over her shoulder very much as the model in Vermeer's *Girl with a Pearl Earring* posed for Vermeer, and in that hour through a precise number of carefully calibrated gestures I re-created Oprah Winfrey's truth as a gift to her for having discovered my own truth; and then once having learned the gestures, I repeated them again and again, in a ritual act to bring back to life in my own studio Oprah Winfrey who glimmered in-visibly on the stool emitting a blue spectral light within the bubble of that circle drawing, asking me to close the gap of periapsis that still drifted between us.

I had become so obsessed with learning what I have subsequently called "the ritual of my Oprah gestures" that I failed at first to notice that midway through that sequence of gestures there was an absolutely unthinking yet beautifully fluid gesture that formed unbelievably, a perfect O. As far as I know, Gideon, in my life as an artist and in all of the years of my art-making, I had never created through a single unthinking gesture a perfect O. And yet here I was moving fluidly through the full sequence of my Oprah gestures, and there it was, again and again, that beautifully fluid gesture that lay in the middle sequence of my Oprah gestures and with charcoal pencil in hand it formed miraculously a perfect "O." O for ovum. O for egg. O for Oprah. O for morning or evening sun that rises askance to the horizon line, flooding the zone with light. O for the zero that I felt I was when I wasn't in my studio working. O for the totality of Oprah's comprehension of who I was and of who I wasn't. I also noticed, quite coincidentally, that the mark that I made on my large canvas when I was startled by the ringing of my studio bell on the day that Oprah visited me formed a perfect O. I had been startled out of my concentration and that O registered both the depth of my concentration at the moment the bell to my studio rang and the full range of my startlement, and the two—the concentration and the startlement— created in paint a perfect circle on my canvas and I knew it was a perfect circle because I later measured the circumference of that circle and divided it by its diameter and I discovered indeed that the ratio came out exactly to the endless numerical iteration that is π, proving, therefore, that my O was a perfect circle. I had calculated the ratio of my diameter as I measured it against the circumference of my circle; I had calculated it out to its hundredth decimal point which, vast as that decimal calculation was, was itself a nothing against the infinite number of decimal points that endlessly fell into the abyss of π's own endlessness . . .

It was then that I realized that Oprah's own runic code and the endlessness of her mystery was related to the ratio of the circumference of a circle to its diameter; in other words, Oprah was as infinite and all-encompassing as was π! And what is π but a regressive asymptotic infinity; a circle spinning endlessly around its own horizon line spewing out a random set of numbers whose collective endless wholeness spoke in the deepest sense to the most perfect ordering of the thing itself, the thing that is Oprah that no one else sees, she, whose ordering is the beautiful luminous blue light behind the veil of the charcoal pencil; she, the thing itself behind all other things that it is yet the thing. It was this small gap, not the three units of her diameter but the endless asymptotic decimalization into the abyss that she called me to fall into and then to describe in my drawing and I fell down into the gap between the embracing arms that as they embraced could still not quite touch, into the embouchure of the mouth as it closes to produce a whistle, the gap of the still-closing lips which as they close produce the sibilant of a kiss, the gap through which the kiss is made, come closer, come closer still, please close the gap of periapsis that falls between us, gaze into the tunnels of my eyes and be lost in a windblown world of breaking hopes and a shipwrecked country of green blue dreams, which itself seems to me to be the sibilant sound of privacy whispering like the wind through the gap … it was here, Gideon, in that small aperture of π where I felt I had encountered the entryway into the unseen private world of Oprah Winfrey. You can't create a perfect circle out of three diameters but you need the vanishing infinity beyond the decimal to create a perfect and endless O. If the three diameters of the circle form very nearly the circle, then it was this part of Oprah that was exposed for all the world to see, but there remained this small gap of π's decimalization that led into the abyss of her own private world and with this insight, I had felt I had encountered something that no other person with the possible exception of you, Gideon, when you danced with Oprah Winfrey onstage, has encountered. I was struck with awe that Oprah had shown me the way to her and I felt somehow vastly empowered by the knowledge that I had done what Oprah bid me do, I had glimpsed her truth and in so doing, I felt that I had snatched fire from the phoenix; I caught the blue flame of Oprah …

3 . 1 4 1 5 9 2 6 5 3 5 8 9 7 9 3 2 3 8 4 6 2 6 4 3 3 8 3 2 7 9 5
0 2 8 8 4 1 9 7 1 6 9 3 9 9 3 7 5 1 0 5 8 2 0 9 7 4 9 4 4 5 9 2 3
0 7 8 1 6 4 0 6 2 8 6 2 0 8 9 9 8 6 2 8 0 3 4 8 2 5 3 4 2 1 1 7 0
6 7 9 8 2 1 4 8 0 8 6 5 1 3 2 8 2 3 0 6 6 4 7 0 9 3 8 4 4 6 0 9 5
5 0 5 8 2 2 3 1 7 2 5 3 5 9 4 0 8 1 2 8 4 8 1 1 1 7 4 5 0 2 8 4 1
0 2 7 0 1 9 3 8 5 2 1 1 0 5 5 5 9 6 4 4 6 2 2 9 4 8 9 5 4 9 3 0 3
8 1 9 6 4 4 2 8 8 1 0 9 7 5 6 6 5 9 3 3 4 4 6 1 2 8 4 7 5 6 4 8 2
3 3 7 8 6 7 8 3 1 6 5 2 7 1 2 0 1 9 0 9 1 4 5 6 4 8 5 6 6 9 2 3 4
6 0 3 4 8 6 1 0 4 5 4 3 2 6 6 4 8 2 1 3 3 9 3 6 0 7 2 6 0 2 4 9 1
4 1 2 7 3 7 2 4 5 8 7 0 0 6 6 0 6 3 1 5 5 8 8 1 7 4 8 8 1 5 2 0 9
2 0 9 6 2 8 2 9 2 5 4 0 9 1 7 1 5 3 6 4 3 6 7 8 9 2 5 9 0 3 6 0 0
1 1 3 3 0 5 3 0 5 4 8 8 2 0 4 6 6 5 2 1 3 8 4 1 4 6 9

It was then, Gideon, I made a point to get a copy of your book, *Gideon's Confession*, and I read it carefully. I read it as if I were a blind person feeling my way through an archaic runic code of text. I read each letter of every word as if those letters themselves were your own private runes that somehow spoke the secret seed of you, and I considered both the letter and the words that you had written, carefully; I read the sentences and paragraphs; I studied the text carefully. I read and reread your book at different times of day. I read your book in the morning and I read it at night. I read your book when sunshine was filtering into my studio at its brightest zenith of the day and I read it while the full moon overhead filled my studio with its cold reflection of the sun's glow; I read your book in the calmness of the hour and I read it while my windows were battered by the gale force winds that Chicago is famous for. I read your text so many times, attempting to bring the fullness of the text into my body. I started to memorize sections of your text so that while I went through the full range of my ritual Oprah gestures, pursuing thus the new direction my art had taken subsequent to Oprah's visit to my studio, I could say over to myself the words that you, Gideon, had written in your book. Repetitious readings of textual fragments in your book helped me better understand those words but the repetitions themselves helped drain meaning from the text so that the repetitions of the text became a ritualized formality that put me into an incantatory state and in such a state I would incant your words either in the most private whisper to myself or sometimes in a loud chanting incantatory voice. I tried to bring your words, Gideon, so completely into me that at times while I performed a set of ritualized Oprah gestures and while I repeated sections of text that you had written in your book, I felt that I myself, and not you, were the author of the text I was reciting. As Hamlet remarked to the Players, Speak the speech, I pray you, as I pronounce it to you, trippingly on the tongue. Remember that Hamlet himself was not the author of his words but Shakespeare, though Hamlet spoke them as if he were the author of his words. So too am I a Hamlet relative to the words that you, Gideon, wrote in your book, *Gideon's Confession*.

I've read your book so many times now, Gideon, that I've committed to my memory vast tracts of your writing and rather than your disappointment and shame at having written and published such a book, I think you should be happy that you wrote that book. If anything, your book has spoken to me about my own calling as an artist more than just about any other book that I have read. For instance, do you remember writing these words which I can recite to you from memory as if they were brand-new words spoken by me for the first time:

THE MORNING SUN was beautiful on the lake's horizon. It raised its heavy head—fierce, lionlike. Have you ever stood close to a lion pacing inside its cage? I have, and I was terrified, thinking, What if my bowels should be suddenly ripped open? I have also looked into the mouth of that same lion while it opened and roared, and I felt a primitive fear that made me leap back in terror. I felt that way now, before the rising sun—awed, terrified.

There was a man a stone's throw away from me. He too stood facing the rising sun, stretching, doing his tai chi exercises. I imagined he thought the sun rose because he invited it to do so. I stood with my hands in my pockets wondering what on earth would become of me. I felt loved but aimless. I felt hopeful but despairing. I felt healthy but on the verge of self-destruction.

After I had read this in your book, Gideon, which by the way, is a remarkably beautiful and powerful bit of writing about being open to the savage power of light and of the sun, a savage power that I in my own practice as an artist always try to confront as honestly as I am able to, after I had absorbed this bit of writing of yours which showed me a pathway to my own truthful confrontation of my own lions, in this case, the lion that was the Oprah who visited me each day sitting in ghostly similitude upon the stool in my studio, I began to follow a new framework for my own art practice. I started the morning not with the ritualized tai chi gestures that you referenced that man doing in the morning as the sun rose above the lake's horizon; instead, I started performing the exact sequence of my Oprah gestures with the same care as that man must have taken as he performed his tai chi motions in front of the rising sun. I would proceed through the ritual of my Oprah gestures working from the exact position, let's call it the chancel, where I was when I drew the first Oprah drawing and facing the empty stool that Oprah had positioned herself on and which stood on a slightly elevated stage, let's call it the altar, and going through that set of ritual gestures I entered into a sort of strange priestly state where that set of ritual gestures in the brightly illuminated space of my studio would conjure yet again Oprah Winfrey on her stool thereby confirming her promise, *I will be back*, even though I knew that she would never be back in my studio in person but only in spirit, but confirming that as long as I performed my set of ritual gestures she, Oprah Winfrey, would appear in a round bubble of blue radiance very much like that model who sat for Vermeer in the famous painting *Girl with a Pearl Earring*, and while she, Oprah, sat for me, in the full range of her myriad and manifold meanings she would urge me to close the gap of the periapsis between her ghostly orbit and mine, and in that moment I would fall yet again into the endless infinity of her green blue dreams.

I stayed with the charcoal pencil for many months, and while the seasons created different configurations of light flowing through the aperture of my studio windows, I was still able each day to render from the charcoal drawings a low blue illumination that was inherent to the drawing itself and glowed behind the black charcoal that my ritual gestures had imparted to the paper. Once I had fully mastered the gestural sequence of my Oprah gestures I began to experiment with different media. Naturally, the painting that I had been working on the day Oprah rang the bell to my studio and startled me from my work, that painting with the perfect O began to draw my attention. It was the last thing I had done as an artist prior to my own perturbation brought on by Oprah's visit. There had been a tremor, the ringing of the bell to my studio, then an earthquake, the visit of Oprah Winfrey to my studio, and then the opening of a fault line which occurred the moment Oprah left my studio, a fault line that had itself created an almost unbridgeable gap between the artist that I was prior to Oprah's visit and the artist that I became after

Oprah's visit and looking at that canvas with the perfect O on it, which was part of my nine-by-nine black and white diptych series, I couldn't help but feel a tender nostalgia for that person and artist who I once was in the hermetic anonymity of my own becoming because now, after Oprah's visit I felt the burden of my responsibility as a person and as an artist to maintain and preserve with ritual perfection the gestural sequence of hand movements that had led to the creation of that first Oprah drawing.

I was now an artist who had two different parts to my career. There was the artist and artwork that I had painted prior to my visit by Oprah Winfrey and there was the artist and artwork that I had painted after my visit by Oprah Winfrey. Before Oprah visited me that day by stealth and rang my bell I was an artist working on large-scale black and white diptych paintings and following my brushstrokes, I attempted to find the bliss of my own eternity at the joining place where the paint touched the canvas, but after Oprah's visit I became the sole priest and master of a singular set of ritual gestures which had the power to conjure from the ether Oprah Winfrey in her full lionlike radiance of awe-inspiring truthfulness, and in so doing, I was able to impart residual radiant blue emanations from the material objects that I, with brush or pencil in hand, had performed my ritual gestures against.

The before moment of my career where I worked as a painter in the anonymity of my own becoming, shall we call it my Eden, and my after moment, shall we call it my fall from grace. I can see now that my Eden was as beautiful as Eden could be.

Those were the best years of my life as a painter. They weren't totally anonymous either, because Gideon, unlike you who wanted to forget absolutely everything having to do with your experience at the University of Chicago, I only wanted to remove myself a few miles away to the Chinatown location so as to reduce the influence of the University of Chicago on my work. Nevertheless, I had remained quite friendly with my former art professor, Gwendolyn Davis. She encouraged me to pursue my obsession to paint the sun as it emerged and fell beneath the horizon line thereby flooding or draining the zone with light and what's more, she encouraged me to put my work out into the world where it belonged, but I never set out to become an artist in the traditional sense nor did I want to participate in the so-called art scene. I only wanted to make art, I didn't want to make a reputation and display and sell my paintings, and since my father was rich, he was able to fund me in my quixotic journey. I rented storage space from an adjacent Chinatown warehouse to store my paintings and I kept meticulous records on the material properties and compositional methods that went into each painting along with the dates of each painting's composition, then I ordered all of my paintings chronologically in my storage vault and if I wasn't organizing my paintings in my storage vault, I was in my studio making more paintings, and when I wasn't making paintings, I was organizing my storage vault, and when I wasn't either organizing my storage vault or making my paintings then I wandered about the Chinatown neighborhood feeling like I was a zero and a nothing and a nonentity and a person who was a nobody of no worth and then when these feelings of worthlessness became unbearable I would find my way back into my studio or into my storage space working one way or another on my artwork wherein I attempted to discover the bliss of my own eternity.

Once in a while, Gwendolyn Davis would show up to my studio with friends of hers and though I didn't actively seek out an audience for my work I was also not averse to having visitors to my studio especially if they were friends of Gwendolyn's and in this way and from all of these visits of these different people laterally or directly connected to the art world, a small reputation started to collect around me and my artwork. I became affectionately known as the Hermit of 16th Street, and my studio, which was becoming a small gathering hub for people interested in observing my methods, was colloquially known as the Bell Jar because that's what Gwendolyn called it and she liked to point out how my paintings were inspired by antecedents as diverse as the late swamp paintings of George Inness Jr. or the water lilies of Monet or the late great seascapes of J.M.W. Turner, and she, Gideon, I'll have you know, made the exact same connections of my paintings to their lineal antecedents that you so insightfully made, but Gwendolyn would talk me up to her friends as I pulled the paintings out of my storage vault and she would point out how my paintings invariably extended the conversation of how a body of work predicated upon those earlier masters could still find the power to say something indelible and new, and she termed what I was doing "a new moment of erotically charged feminized neo-Expressionism"—a clunky school if I ever heard one so named, and a name that came too uncomfortably close to something that my work definitely wasn't, erotically charged feminized neo-Nazism, but Gwendolyn's category of thought and her way of talking about what I was trying to do in my work, for she, as a supreme conceptual artist, was exceptionally eloquent while talking about someone else's art practice—remember she used to say *Kung fu the bell jar*—but she helped frame what I was doing for those who were experiencing it for the first time and with that framing they were then able to start to verbalize and categorize the raw emotional impact that my art was having upon them and I witnessed again and again the stupefaction that my artwork induced upon the sensibilities of those who were looking at it and I felt it yet again, how my paintings with their own peculiar bewitchments had switched the gaze that might have otherwise fallen upon me to my actual paintings and I felt tremendous consolation in that. The wayward location of my studio in the Chinatown warehouse district on the western bank of the Chicago River with the St. Charles Air Line Bridge, a structural steel and concrete immensity that filled the view of my lower studio windows, the strangeness of all of this and the bewitching work that I was then doing, and my unwillingness to show my work except to those who visited my studio, all of these things combined to make my studio a sort of pilgrimage destination for a small coterie of art cognoscenti, and surrounded by my paintings we all collectively seemed to find the bliss of our own eternity. And this arrangement, Gideon, my near total solitary confinement in my studio obsessively painting my canvases, and the random and infrequent visits from a small clutch of admirers who, through their various writings that they were publishing in the art journals about my work thereby making known to the broader group of art cognoscenti what it was that I was doing in my own art practice, all of this was enough to sustain me, and it made me as happy as I thought possible. I was in my own Eden and I was so happy in my work that I didn't even consider the fact that there might be a serpent lurking in the garden of my solitary rapture, but the serpent, wherever it was, and I didn't know this at the time, but the serpent was closer to my door than I had imagined. And then you, Gideon, published your book and you divulged privacies that I had inadvertently shared with you, and your book blew up and went viral, and it began to change the cultural conversation around our generation, and then you showed up on *The Oprah Winfrey Show* and you did your little dance with Oprah and then, because your book was so accurate in its depiction of where my studio had been and because what you had written about me stirred the interest of Oprah Winfrey, the serpent, which I didn't know at the time was a serpent, the serpent had shown up outside the door of my studio, and ringing my bell, Oprah Winfrey to my surprise showed up in my studio, and not only did she apprehend absolutely and totally what my paintings were about, but she also apprehended why I, Regina Blast, had become the so-called Hermit of 16th Street, even though she didn't in fact know that I was sometimes called the Hermit of 16th Street, but she understood absolutely the causes of my hermeticism and her understanding of me was so absolute and complete that she gasped when she saw my diptych paintings and she described with even greater precision what my paintings were attempting to do than the art critics who had been writing about me in the journals were able to do, and her understanding of my artwork at that time only rivaled your understanding, Gideon, but in addition to her understanding of my artwork she also understood who I was and who I wasn't and her apprehension of me in my totality of being and nonbeing was absolute and that's when she, Oprah, asked me to draw her and to find by drawing her the Oprah that no one on Earth had ever seen. That was the moment gazing into the tunnels of her eyes when I was lost in a windblown world of breaking hopes and a shipwrecked country of green blue dreams and while I fell down into the small and endless gap of π's infinitude I invented the set of gestures which became my ritualized Oprah gestures and by discovering these gestures, I began to embark on an entirely new model of art production that was totally unrelated to all that other work that had precursed my Oprah perturbation, it was as if those paintings painted in the Eden of my own becoming had fallen like angels into the hell of their own irrelevancy, the light that they formerly seemed to embody, seemed, after my Oprah perturbation, to be switched off, and rather than the glowingly alive paintings that I thought I had made and stored in my Chinatown vault, I only saw dull and darkened pictures that no longer had the vigor to sustain a moment's observation.

But that didn't matter because now I had become sole priest and master of the ritualized Oprah gestures and as I performed these sets of gestures with a charcoal pencil or paintbrush in hand rendering an image from those ritual-ized gestures, I had not only conjured Oprah Winfrey as she sat in the ghostly orb of blue radiance, poised in a serpentine position around the vertical axis looking over her shoulder at me as if she were the model of Vermeer's famous painting *Girl with a Pearl Earring*, but I was also able to conjure that thing that Oprah is, that no one else sees, she, whose order-ing is the beautiful luminous blue light behind the veil of the charcoal pencil; she, the thing itself behind all other things that it is yet the thing. I performed these gestures and I incanted from memory sections of your text and whatever were the final words that I would incant from your text as I finished up my ritualized gestures, I would then, like William Blake, write these words on the object, the paper, or the canvas, or even lately, the wet terra-cotta that I had performed my ritual gestures against, and so a new production of artwork started to emerge from my studio. There was a growing set of images that was a repetition of the first image that I had made of Oprah while she was in my studio and a bit of text would fall on each of these images; text that was either from the words that had entered my head when I first saw Oprah, or fragments of text from your book. For instance, these are some of the sayings that I have recorded on my ritual Oprah art, in the way that William Blake recorded his innermost thoughts on his visionary work:

1. "She wore jackboots, had butch hair, and sported a sleeveless T-shirt with army surplus cargo pants."
2. "She was fat, with a big round ass. Tattoos of names and numbers—algebra, calculus, a shibboleth of numeric data that added up to some algorithm with runic import—proliferated in inky darkness across the canvas of her body."
3. "Gaze into the tunnels of my eyes and be lost in a windblown world of breaking hopes and a shipwrecked country of green blue dreams . . ."
4. "She had a ring in her nose as well, which I tugged."
5. "I watched her shake and giggle and it made me giggle, and it was by giggling and jiggling that we passed the

rest of the afternoon in the light of those glorious
paintings."

6. "Gaze into the tunnels of my eyes and be lost in a
windblown world of breaking hopes and a shipwrecked
country of green blue dreams . . ."

7. "I want you to fuck me silly. I want you to fuck me until my eyeballs roll around in my head. I want you to
fuck me until a beam of light comes shooting out of my
mouth. Do you think you can do that for me?"

8. "She painted huge canvases of empty rooms filled with
the most beautiful light imaginable. It was a 'light at the
end of the tunnel' kind of light. A 'light that you see
when you die and go to heaven' kind of light."

9. "Ask her what she painted, and she'd tell you, I paint
light. But when you saw one of her pictures it was clear
she was attempting nothing short of depicting some sort
of celestial bliss."

10. "Gaze into the tunnels of my eyes and be lost in a windblown world of breaking hopes and a shipwrecked country of green blue dreams . . ."

11. "The beauty of the light in her pictures was so urgent
and raw, it produced a lump in my throat."

12. "The number π is a mathematical constant, approxi-
mately equal to 3.14159. It is defined in Euclidean
geometry as the ratio of a circle's circumference to its
diameter."

13. "It was this small gap, not the three units of her diameter but the endless asymptotic decimalization into the
abyss that she called me to fall into and then to describe
in my drawing and I fell down into the gap between

the embracing arms that as they embraced could still
not quite touch, into the embouchure of the mouth as
it closes to produce a whistle, the gap of the still-closing
lips which as they close produce the sibilant of a kiss,
the gap through which the kiss is made, come closer,
come closer still . . ."

And so it went, Gideon, my new art practice. I had entered
a new dawn, and I painted a different star. I was no longer
painting the sun as it sat askance to the horizon line, rather
I did my own set of gestures, what Gwendolyn Davis, when
she first started to watch me perform in my new art practice
described as Kabuki theater. Regina, your gestures, my art
teacher Gwendolyn Davis said to me, are like Kabuki theater
and as such they are your artwork. This object which records
the fluid gestures of your ritual motions is part of your art,
but it is not the whole part of your art. The whole part of
your art includes the churchlike studio space where you conduct your priestly gestures in the different valuations of light
that filter through the aperture of your glass-domed studio;
the gestures themselves as you conduct them in a precisely
regulated sequence; the utterances that I hear you make in-
canting words and phrases that you have committed to memory and which in a final flourish you transmit in writing to
the object that you are working upon, and the full range of
objects that fulfill your art practice: the brush or pencil or
trowel; the materials: the paint, or charcoal, and the canvases,
papers, and terra-cotta formations which of late you have applied your gestural sequence to. You are no longer a painter,
Regina Blast. You have become a conceptual artist and you

have aestheticized a set of ritual gestures and those gestures are the gestures of a painter making a painting, but this insight of yours that a set of ritual gestures, the painter's gestural motions as the painter makes a painting, as well as the actual tracings that your gestures leave upon a receptive object, these ideas of yours that you are showing me in your practice are a genuine contribution. It's as if, for instance, to take Matisse and his painting *Girl in Yellow and Blue with Guitar*, as a case in point, but your work aestheticizes the gestural motions of the painter as the painter paints into a set of ritual objects, the point that not just the painting of Matisse the painter is the whole work of art, but as if, and if only, his hand movements as he painted *Girl in Yellow and Blue with Guitar*, had been preserved, but they too would be an indelible part of the artwork *Girl in Yellow and Blue with Guitar*. Gwendolyn Davis's aha moment relative to my new art practices set in motion my new artistic phase.

Once my old professor, Gwendolyn Davis, had started to see the whole component of my art-making, she brought her friends to see what I was doing and slowly, over time, we turned my studio space into an art production studio whose focus became both the so-called Kabuki theater of my ritualized Oprah gestures and the material objects that I imparted my gestures to and we started to film my process and the films of my process became part of the artwork as well. We set tripod video cameras to form an equilateral triangle around the perimeter of my gallery space with the centroid, O, where the medians of the equilateral triangle met, exactly set to match the spot of the stool where Oprah Winfrey had sat on the altar that day in my studio staring at me over her shoulder as if she were a model in Vermeer's painting *Girl with a Pearl Earring*, and from my position at the chancel I conducted my set of ritualized gestures. We randomized the filming of my gestures from camera to camera by creating π segmentations of time. Each camera would film for thirty seconds my performative ritual gestures and then the filming would switch to the next camera for thirty seconds and then the next, and once the set of three cameras had filmed for thirty seconds we created a gap of time equal to π's decimalization and during that moment, the filming would switch to a camera that was positioned above the stool, and filming down for that brief moment of time, it would capture in the studio space where Oprah had sat and which invariably radiated a blue prismatic light of astonishing beauty. These cameras which formed a tetrahedron or rather a triangular pyramid and the rotating videos coming from each corner of the tetrahedron filmed in time signatures equal to π with the topmost camera producing the time segmentation as closely as we could approximate it to π's infinite decimalization capturing the violet and blue colors that effloresced in a luminous orblike sphere as I conducted my ritualized Oprah gestures; these things combined with the material objects that I had imparted the tracings of my ritual gestures to became the installation model that formed the new basis of my art career.

Maybe you've been to one of my art installations, Gideon? They've appeared in museums and studio spaces throughout the world. I've made a living of it, and as Claire mentioned in that letter she wrote to you, I've received a bit of acclaim and notoriety, but none of this would have happened had you not written so vividly about me and my artwork in your book, and certainly none of this would have happened had not Oprah Winfrey rung my studio bell that afternoon so long ago, startling me from my work. I don't know whether to say *thank you* or *I hate you* for what you have done. Left to my own devices I might still be trying to find the bliss of my own eternity in the solitude of my studio, in the anonymity of my own becoming, making paintings of the sun's luminescence as it filters through the windows of my studio. But there was a rupture and I've broken away from that earlier art practice.

I hope you can say thank you to me, I told Regina.

I want to hate you, Gideon.

You can hate me as well, I told her.

I'll thank you instead, she said, and then she smiled at me and I was returned to that moment seventeen years ago when I was still dating Claire and when I had first locked eyes with Regina, and I knew then as I knew now that I was looking into the eyes of the only person I had ever met who cared enough about who I was to be both open to who I was as a person and brutally honest with what she saw when she was taking me in with those large dark eyes of hers.

Thank you too, I told her. And I'm sorry for what I did.

I accept your apology.

And then we hugged. And then she said, I hope you don't ever betray me again.

B efore Regina left me that morning she said, Gideon, it was so nice seeing you and talking to you this morning. I don't often see old friends and seeing you here this morning just brought something out of me. I hope that this strange confession that we made to each other can stay between us. I hope that this is a privacy, our mutual perturbations of O, that we can share between ourselves, and sharing this privacy we can be bound forever whether or not we see each other again, for we will always have the memory of our talk, and the knowledge that neither you nor I are alone because of the intense and private experiences we have shared with each other and because we both have knowledge of something no one else in the world has, we possess an intimate experience with that rarest glimpsed thing, the private Oprah Winfrey.

Regina looked at me with such warmth and kindness in her face and suddenly we hugged and then she gave me a long passionate kiss and though I myself never felt loved in the way that someone might make another person feel loved by giving that person a long passionate kiss, yet that morning, in Regina Blast's embrace, and in the tenderness of her kiss I felt the bliss of my own eternity which was really just the special magic of Regina imparting the bliss of her own eternity upon me. Then, smiling, but still holding me in her embrace we did a small impromptu dance. If I remember correctly, Gideon, this was the dance that you performed with Oprah. Am I right about this? I felt the sway of Regina's body and I moved with her sway so that a small gap of private space opened and closed gently between us, *That's right* I said without saying it. *This is exactly the dance that I had with Oprah.* I danced Regina out the door of the coffee shop and then a moment later she got in her car, as she drove past me, she rolled down her window, waved. There was that mirthful smile again that reminded me of the first moment seventeen years ago I first set eyes on her, and that look of hers that saw straight through me and seemed to completely understand who I was. *Okay. Goodbye, Mr. King of Slack! Remember, this is our secret! Let's keep it between ourselves this time.* And then she was gone. I have never seen her again.

I stood near the garden with the magnolia tree in full bloom in the noon light of a radiant spring day, holding the manuscript of the book that I had meant to read so that I could blurb it, a manuscript which didn't have a title but which the author had called the man/dog/cure book. I clutched the book under my arm and I thought about all the ways that we live in the world. Here was a person, the Kentucky gentleman's grandson who had penned a manuscript about his years-long battle with chronic illness that was only abated when he discovered quite by accident that the runt of a litter, a small beagle dog whom he had named Beatrice, could take his mind off his pain by merely wagging its tail and howling. I wrote a book called *The Ark of Disquiet*, which, if nothing else, was a howl of pain directed at the cosmos. It was a private book, *The Ark of Disquiet*, meant only for me, and yet I had wandered out of my own quietude and urged on by that Kentucky gentleman and my subsequent literary agent, I was encouraged to publish it under the title *Gideon's Confession*, and so named, my small confession whose sole audience was me found its way like a small boat wending its way down a small stream into the open water of acclaim and fame that it was destined to have. I kept wanting to tell people who asked me about the book and how I came to write it, people who looked to me as if I might know something about them and thereby help them, that though you think this is my so-called confession which I have delivered to you, the reader, as if I were a supplicant looking to absolve myself of whatever a confession to an anonymous reader might absolve me of, in fact it wasn't a confession nor was it designed to be a confession. When it was written, I had called it *The Ark of Disquiet*, and I don't know why I wrote *The Ark of Disquiet*, I only know that I wrote it in an attempt to cure myself of a year, my final year, at the University of Chicago that had, for some inexplicable reason, filled me completely with bile and made me want to puke and the writing of *The Ark of Disquiet* was in effect my mode of vomit; it was my cleansing. But what was I attempting to cleanse myself of? I told Regina and anyone else who would listen that I wanted absolutely and categorically to forget everyone and everything that happened to me during my final year at the University of Chicago and that's why I wrote the book, but this still didn't answer for me or for anyone else why I, a fourth-year student at the University of Chicago, who was estranged from my ambitious father and from my equally ambitious brothers but I had nevertheless found an unlikely sponsor in my maternal uncle, a man whom I referred to as Unc, and who bequeathed upon me a generous monthly stipend to help me get along in the world, but why did I, under those conditions, want to forget everything? What was there to forget? I was unloved, yes. But why had I been unloved, why did I feel unloved and why did it take my little dance with Oprah Winfrey on the stage of her show, our two bodies gently swaying together, why did it take that dance to alert me at least to the causes of my unlovedness that led to the writing of my book? Why was I so unloved? Was it because I myself was somehow marked as unlovable? There had been malign forces all throughout my life that had caused me pain, there were people, there were relationships, I had felt entrenched and locked into a social identity which I detested. I felt like a small-town boy who didn't know how to get out of town; only I wasn't a small-town boy, I was a fourth-year college student at the University of Chicago, and when I wasn't sitting in on classes I was hiding from the world at a small neighborhood tavern getting consoled by my friend Vic, the old bartender who counseled me on life and whose counsel I took very seriously, but I was stuck and this being stuck caused me pain, so I tried to write it all down, I tried to describe the relationships, my situational stasis, my horror of having to find the ambition gene which I somehow lacked but which my brothers possessed, and what I seemed to have instead, was what my agent had first identified as the indolence gene, *your indolence gene* he said, and maybe it's not just your indolence gene, but maybe, just maybe it is a gene that has infected a large population of kids from your generation, and if I am right about this, my agent said, then we will find out soon enough because if your indolence gene which infects your manuscript is a gene that also infects your generation, then it's a long shot but not impossible that your book may become the literary anthem of your generation, and my agent proved to be prescient. My whole generation was infected by the indolence gene. We were the last generation in human history who had spent our childhoods free of any awareness of computers, we lived our youth in an innocent splendor of weedy fields and willow trees, we had no way of knowing, in our innocence, that the world was just moments away from changing forever, and the first-generation Apple computer that I had typed my handwritten manuscript into, *The Ark of Disquiet*, that ancient computer was the harbinger of the change, it was the hinge upon which the door swang open to a digitally connected cybernetic world; there was the before, the weedy fields and willow trees, the wilderness of our own unfoundedness, and there was the after, the hyper-connected cybernetic universe that had garbled the analog world and changed all of us forever and we all walked wit-lessly through that door and stared at the wonder of it, this brand-new cybernetic world, but the staring was away from the world proper, the analog world itself, the weedy fields and willow trees, our own interior privacies, and we moved our attention from the thing itself to its digitization made pos-sible by electronic circuitry and internet connectedness and all that the twenty-first century, our digitized century would bring to us, not least of which was the sense that we were no longer part of the long chain of human history that preceded us. We had knowledge of something our ancestors had no knowledge of, for one we had become cyborgs and we were as a result privy to what that all meant, but they, our pre-cyborg ancestors, had knowledge which was fading rapidly from memory, they knew what it was like to stand in the garden and live in the simple innocence of the analog world with all of their experiences unmitigated by computer technology, but we, my generation, which was soon to become the first cyborg generation, we had the indolence gene that my book, *Gideon's Confession*, had been infected by, and maybe we were indolent not because we lacked ambition but because we wanted to stretch that final hiatus before the computer world hit, we wanted to stretch out the final moments of all those unknowing generations that had preceded us a moment longer. We wanted to linger just a bit in the glorious garden of our own anonymity or maybe it was just me who wanted to linger a bit lost in an analog world of analog memories and of friendships and conversations conducted in the unrecorded now, and maybe my writing of *The Ark of Disquiet* was a sort of temper tantrum that I had thrown because maybe I had sensed that wild ambition was taking us inexorably forward out of the garden of our own unfoundedness and I was mad about that; my anger—what's the hurry, can't we stay a moment longer in this lovely garden!—this anger infused every word of my book. First I wrote in longhand *The Ark of Disquiet*, wherein I had shepherded all the creatures of my discontent, then I had typed into a first-generation Apple computer *The Ark of Disquiet*. Next I was going to print my manuscript onto paper so that I could hurl the manuscript like a turd into the waves of a storm-tossed Lake Michigan, and then I was going to return to my apartment to destroy the floppy disk that the manuscript had been saved on. I should have destroyed that Apple computer instead. But I kept the computer, and I kept the floppy disk, and when I printed up my manuscript, I sent it instead to the Kentucky gentleman's agent.

Who am I and what am I? For a long time I didn't have an answer to either of these questions. I myself felt myself to be an endless nothing not worthy of the friendship I received or of the goodwill checks that Unc mailed to me to string me along from day to day while I attempted to conduct my life from the barstool of a run-down local tavern. My book, which was my cri de coeur, that is to say that it represented a profound crisis of my own heart, had, after I had written it, no more value to me than a turd, and by calling my cri de coeur not the red-alert-existential-statement that it in fact was, but calling it, the manuscript, and all of the thoughts and feelings contained therein, "a turd" that night while I was having drinks with that Kentucky gentleman who would later become one of my most valued friends, I had, by demoting my book to a turd, elevated it in the eyes of that Kentucky gentleman, who told me that very night, albeit drunkenly, that my book, Your book, he said, if it had any value at all was "directly" correlative to the fact that rather than being the cri de coeur that so many memoirs so definitely are, that yours, tongue-in-cheek, was in fact a turd and because it was a turd, he continued on in his drunken state, then your book must be published rather than wasted in the storm-tossed waters of Lake Michigan, because, and this is what he said to me, his face coming leeringly close to mine, he said: It is because your memoir is a turd that it should be published, because that is what differentiates it from all the other shite that's published these days, and by publishing your turd if you should choose to do so, you will have a golden opportunity to raise your fuck-you finger to the world and tell them all to eat shit motherfuckers! They deserve nothing less. And so I took him up on it, and my book was published not as *The Ark of Disquiet* but as *Gideon's Confession*, and when it was published I said to my agent, so there it is. My book has been published, to which my agent said to me, Congratulations! And I turned and asked him, What are you congratulating me for? And he told me, I am congratulating you on the occasion of the publication of your book. To which I told him, Please don't congratulate me for that, congratulate me instead because my book is my fuck-you finger to the world, congratulate me because with the publication of this book, I am telling the world with all of its motherfuckers to eat shit and die! To which my agent, who still at that moment didn't think that there was any prospect in the publication of my book, said, Congratulations, then, for that as well. It was only later, and sooner than we thought, when the money would start to roll in. There were the reviews; the grand statements that my book was the "bible of the Slacker Generation," and of course, there was the two-step dance that I performed with Oprah in plain sight for all the world to see; following which there was the Broadway musical and the cult movie, *The Slacker King*; and then there were all of the assholes whom I wanted to brand forever as assholes who wanted to brand me as their friend, just as all of my friends whom I wanted to brand as friends only branded me as an asshole. And then there were the paparazzi and the endless stupid fame, the endlessly debated and ridiculous question splashed on the pages of all the gossip rags: Was I or was I not Oprah's objet d'amour? And then there were all of the various printings and reprintings and the repackaging and the rebranding and all the new editions of my book, *Gideon's Confession*, and all of the different lists, those all-important lists, that proclaimed my book as essential reading if you wanted to understand Generation Slacker, or if you wanted to understand our era and its discontents, or even, as some lists claimed, if you wanted to understand where America was situated at a perilous moment of time just as its own pre-2K innocence was rapidly coming to an end, its so-called blithe and happy ignorance before the digitally connected cyborg wave of twenty-first-century computing technology crashed down on human history putting forever into the past the strange human behavior, whatever that might have been, when there wasn't a computer available to distract human attention away from the world and toward the screen. What was that prehistory and what had humans done then with all the time that they had at their disposal because there were no screens to look at? And I imagine all of the extra time humans, myself included, must have spent in the stillness of the garden trying to capture the radiance of the world as it filtered through the leaves and flower petals through our retinas and unmitigated by distraction straight into the deepest wells of our souls. In so many ways my book was a success as was I, but in the most primal and intimate way, publication of my book was a catastrophic failure. Publication of *The Ark of Disquiet* did not end my disquiet, nor did it obliviate the year of experience that it was designed to obliviate. It only made public my own privacies for all the world to see and trample upon and to laugh at and to lampoon in the subsequent Broadway musical and cult-classic movie; my own privacies with all of their interior convolutions had in effect become an artifice for the world to project upon it whatever it wished to project. Publication of my book turned my own interiority into a public forum for all who would peer into its pages. Who was the turd here if not I?

It wasn't long after my startling conversation with Regina Blast when I was at another crowded dinner party and I took my accustomed seat next to my friend, the old Kentucky gentleman, and after we had gotten massively drunk on old-fashioneds, I told him of my encounter with Regina. I told him the whole story. I told him how I had been hiding out in a café and how I was preparing to read his grandson's manuscript, *man/dog/cure*, so that I could blurb it. I told him how someone tapped my shoulder disturbing me from a quiet meditation and how with that small tapping Regina Blast had awoken me to myself and to her. Regina saw straight through me, I told the old Kentucky gentleman, and when she saw what she saw, when she saw that indeed all I was was a "turd" she did not flinch, rather she was able to communicate to me with her unflinching stare that not only did she recognize that I was a turd and that I would always only be a turd but she also didn't flinch at this recognition, it was almost as if she saw me for who I was and she had accepted me. Something I've been missing in my life, I told the Kentucky gentleman, is the sense that people are unable to get a direct read on me. I don't know how I appear to the world but the reflection of me that the world sends back to me invariably seems distorted and off the mark. I often felt I was lost in a fun house without an exit surrounded by a bunch of maniacs screaming and laughing at me, but that morning in the coffee shop, I felt that this old friend from the past who knew me before all this crazy fame stuff had overwhelmed my life, she was able to look at me as a human being outside the story that the world has endlessly told of me, and seeing me directly she noticed right away that what I really was was a sad and unhappy turd of a person, and I was so grateful for that recognition. I felt for the first time as if I had arrived home just by looking into the unblinking eyes of another person. Regina Blast saw my truth. She got a clear read on me. She saw the garbage dump that was my life, and rather than disgusting her, it made her smile and if I'm not mistaken there was even a little bit of joyful mirth in her smile, and then she handed over to me my banana and my scone and my coffee with cream and extra sugar and we sat down and talked about the seventeen years that had fallen between us since we last saw each other. She knew of the dance number that I did with Oprah Winfrey on her show. She commented to me that my book was, insofar as I portrayed her in the pages of my book, a violation of her privacy. She also told me that because I had seen her naked and because I had described both her tattoos and the sex that we shared when I met her at her studio, there have been occasions in her life when she's encountered men who wanted to repeat the same sexual encounter with her that I had depicted in my book, and she found this to be disgusting. She also told me that I was the one who had first discovered the truth of her as an artist and though this wasn't compensation enough for the act of betrayal that I had committed when I wrote about the tattoo and the sex, nevertheless it was a consolation. But this understanding that I had of her as an artist, that I, a stranger who had literally just stepped out of the rain into her studio, could suddenly stand in front of her bewitching paintings and that I could get so lost in my wonder brought on by her paintings that I had completely forgotten the original impetus of my visit which was, quite frankly, to harken to my own horniness and to act on a hunch that she might be as attracted to me as I was to her. But I lost myself that afternoon in contemplation of her paintings, and I later wrote about her paintings in my book. I wrote about getting lost in the utter beauty of her paintings, of losing my bearings, of falling out of myself and into the world of her art. I wrote of that experience in my book, *Gideon's Confession*, and my writing of my experience of her art in my book was, according to Regina, so accurate an expression of what she was trying to do as an artist that it had caused her to immediately reconsider her decision to become an artist because it was at that moment, just prior to my visit when she had decided that she had already pushed her art as far as it would go and having pushed her talent to its most extreme point, and her talent was both for brushstroke and also for capturing the light as it either pours forth from the horizon at dawn or withdraws from the world as it recedes at dusk, and I had thought she might be an acolyte of J.M.W. Turner's late paintings, but she had told me that as far as she had pushed her talent to render light in its capacity to either flood the zone or recede from the zone depending on whether our star was rising above or falling below the horizon line, that when I had first encountered her artwork that fateful day I had visited her in her studio, she had already come upon the realization that her work to date skated dangerously close to the work of the commercial artist Thomas Kinkade. I worried, Regina had told me, that insofar as I was painting light and insofar as the world had long ago moved away from any serious consideration of painters who still attempted to paint light, that insofar as I was committed to being a painter of light I would have to contend with the true contemporary masters who attempted to paint light by smearing oil paint on canvas and at the time I was practicing my artwork, she told me, the number one painter of light was Thomas Kinkade. That was the direction the painting of light had taken. Thomas Kinkade had lit the way forward, so to speak. He blazed a trail into the shopping mall gallery and he showed that this was the pathway for other painters who desperately wanted to paint light. The future for painters of light wasn't the art studio, or the museum, those places insofar as they were interested in paintings of light had already filled their walls with the great masters of Impressionism; henceforth, if an artist wanted to paint light the artist would find their market and their audience in the mall; and when I, Regina had told me, realized that not only had the commercial artist Thomas Kinkade shown the direction that my career as an artist would take, again this is Regina talking I told the Kentucky gentleman, and I paraphrased for the Kentucky gentleman as follows: she, Regina, told me that if she wanted to proceed as an artist of light, then she had also intuited that even if she had followed Thomas Kinkade into the mall, and her paintings were certainly of a quality that she would indeed find her way into mall galleries if she chose to do so, but even if she chose to follow Thomas Kinkade, she nevertheless realized that she would never be better than Thomas Kinkade. He was the master of light painting for the market that was hungry for paintings of light and should she, Regina, find herself in this market she realized that she would only and always be, as she put it, second fiddle to Thomas Kinkade, and that is, she would be second fiddle only if she were painting at the top of her form. But when I stepped into her studio from the rain that afternoon, and when she saw my reaction to her paintings she realized that I didn't see her paintings as paintings of light but rather I saw them for what they were: ecstatic expressions of joy made manifest by the sensuous and, quite frankly, the erotic quality of her brushstroke, and my way of seeing her paintings was a revelation for her. She accused me of having a boner when I was looking at her paintings, and maybe that was true. I can't remember, but she said that she thought that I was literally put into a state of erotic arousal by her paintings which were just abstract paintings of light, but it was the brushstroke, she said. She was convinced I was being sexually aroused by the sensuous and erotic quality of her brushstroke, and once she realized this, it was as if I had shown her what the exact properties of her paintings were and also what her unique skill as a painter was. You showed me that I was not just a painter of light, Gideon, she told me that afternoon in the coffee shop, but that I was a painter of brushstrokes and this realization turned me on as a painter and I've been fanatically painting brushstrokes ever since. Of course, I told the Kentucky gentleman, when I was done gawking over her paintings, we then promptly had sex and that's what ended the burgeoning relationship that I had had with my then girlfriend, Claire. And after graduation I was so filled with bile that I didn't know what to do and so I penned my book and it was published as *Gideon's Confession* and I did my two-step with Oprah and the rest is history. I call the whole debacle of my life and of Regina's life insofar as it was impacted by the fame brought on by my dance, the perturbation of O.

The perturbation of what? the old Kentucky gentleman asked.

The perturbation of O.

As soon as I said the words "the perturbation of O," that's

when the old Kentucky gentleman snapped his fingers to get the attention of his agent, who was now also my longtime agent, and he said to our agent, Larry, he said, Hey, Larry, I think Gideon Anderson has another best-seller on his hands, and it's a story about his crazy minute of fame that he experienced on *The Oprah Winfrey Show*. And with that endorsement, we were drunk as hell at the time he made it, I woke the next morning and began my long act of betrayal. I wrote down literally every word that I could recall that Regina Blast and I had shared that fateful morning in the coffee shop, and as soon as I finished the manuscript I sent it to my agent, Larry, who in turn sent it to my publisher, Noname Press, and within days I received a contract for my second book titled just as I had written it, *The Perturbation of O*, and after I signed the contract and dropped it off in the mailbox thereby putting me in a legal relationship that gave permission to my publisher to make available for all the world to see the private conversation that Regina Blast and I had shared and that had concerned nothing less than the sharing of the most private privacies between two people who were doomed to never remain private. Then, after the publication of my book *The Perturbation of O*, and after the second, even crazier round of fame that my new book had aroused, including another luncheon with Oprah Winfrey wherein I poked again with my fork at more shrimp scampi in butter sauce and then on her show where we entertained the audience with a reprise of our two-step dance, but after I stepped out of her studio onto Sangamon Street and wandered home dazed at what I had done publishing a second book that I should have never published, I asked myself, who was I to try and perturb the universe? Better to leave well enough alone. Yet I couldn't leave well enough alone, and so I had perturbed the universe. Now all I could do was wait to see what would come. What would happen next? And while I waited in the unsheltered wilderness that had become my life I also waited for the rending and cracking open of the sky. I waited for a howling tempest to fall and punish the land and when the tempest came, I donned my swim trunks, stepped into my flip-flops, and in slashing gusts of wind and pounding rain I headed Lear-like out to the rocks of Promontory Point. A ziggurat of lightning cracked at the agitated bough of a nearby gnarled redbud in full magenta bloom. It was a sign, I thought; a malignant sign, and I leaped . . . nay, rather, I hurled myself like the turd that I most definitely had become onto the storm-tossed waters of Lake Michigan and when I hit, making my big splash in the swell, I knew that I was irrevocably lost at sea.